"Follow me," Mama said. "There's another path that leads out into the woods. I bet that old man or the boy is hiding back behind those trees." She pointed to an overgrown tangle of trees. The three of us inched down the thin path, surrounded by trees, bramble bushes, weeds, and poison ivy. Flies, mosquitoes, and gnats swarmed around our necks and faces. Despite the heat of the August day, I felt my flesh shiver and my left leg cramp, along with cuts, bruises, aches, and stings. My face and neck began to feel like it was on fire, with sharp little cuts from low hanging tree limbs. I felt like screaming from pain. Oddly, my father didn't say much. He acted like he was in charge and that it was his mission to keep control over the situation. Mama kept pushing ahead, as if she knew exactly where she was headed.

MAMA
SOLVES A
MURDER

Nora L. DeLoach

An Original Holloway House Edition
HOLLOWAY HOUSE PUBLISHING COMPANY
LOS ANGELES, CALIFORNIA

Published by
HOLLOWAY HOUSE PUBLISHING COMPANY
8060 Melrose Avenue, Los Angeles, CA 90046

International Standard Book Number 0-87067-741-1
Printed in the United States of America

Cover illustration by Christopher De Gasperi
Cover design by Bill Skurski

MAMA SOLVES
A MURDER

Chapter 1

My mama's name is Grace. Everybody calls her "Candi," like candied sweet potatoes, because of her skin, a golden brown color with yellow undertones that looks as smooth as silk. I think Mama's great beauty is in her eyes. They are oval and clear, and the blacks and whites are pure and separate. Mama weighs about 140 pounds. She exudes a sweetness and warmth that touches something deep inside most people.

Since I've known Mama longer than almost anybody else in town, let me assure you that the similarity between her and candied sweet potatoes is only skin deep.... Trust me, there are times when she isn't as sweet as she looks. Mama can be shrewd and cunning. She has uncanny perception and self control. Her mind is formidable, her beauty is enticing, but I've seen her use either to get in and out of places.

7

Mama is fifty-three and she works as a social worker in the small town of Hampton, South Carolina. While most of the things that arouse the mind don't excite Mama, I've seen her absolutely euphoric when her mind is deducing. She's a self-styled private investigator who sees herself as the romantic loner. Mama enjoys the tedious jobs of digging up bits and pieces until she's solved a mystery. Long ago, I don't remember when, Mama decided that if she could get at the truth of a problem, she would have made a contribution to humankind.

Who am I? My name is Simone. I'm Mama's one and only daughter. She's got two other children, both boys, but they don't get pulled into Mama's adventures like I do. They think they're too smart, but Mama and I have been playing detective since I was a little girl. As a matter of fact, I remember when we got started. Daddy, a career army man, was stationed at Fort Dix, New Jersey. Mama had just finished a conversation with an officer's wife. When the woman left our house, Mama looked at me and said, "Something in the milk ain't clean."

What do you mean?" I asked.

"My antenna tells me that something ain't right about that woman's story."

"What did she say?"

Mama hesitated. "It's not what she said, Simone, but how she said it, and I'm going to find out the truth. Somehow, I know it's what I'm supposed to do."

I didn't understand Mama then, but I believed her. That was the beginning of our game, which had only two rules. First, we would protect each other. Second, we could each always count on the other being around to help out when needed.

I make my living as a paralegal for Mr. Sidney Jacoby, a prominent criminal lawyer in Atlanta. In Mama's opinion, I'm as good as any of Perry Mason's assistants. (*Perry Mason* is Mama's favorite television program.) Whenever Mama finds something that she thinks is worth sleuthing she calls on me, and I'm obliged to join her in the hunt. To be perfectly honest, Mama is my Sherlock Holmes and I'm her Dr. Watson.

It was late in June when Mama called. That Monday a relentless downpour had begun in mid-afternoon. It was the kind of rain that beat the shrubs and flowers so much that the sidewalks and streets became littered with their leaves.

At six o'clock I left the office. Having gathered up a stack of manila folders and dumped them in the back-seat of my car, I drove home through small rivers in the streets. Fortunately, my apartment's parking is covered, so I braved the dampness with an arm full of folders. I sighed. There was no way I could get through all the reading at the office so, as usual, I took work home. After several hours of leafing through page after page of interrogatories and making an occasional note to myself, I put the pieces back together, one section at a time, and placed the stack neatly in the corner of the room.

I was curled up on the couch after having finished off shrimp fried rice generously laden with sweet and sour sauce, hot mustard, and soy sauce. The empty pint carton lay on the coffee table with several pads and pencils. The sound of the water drumming against the window had me wavering between sleep and the voices from the movie on television. The telephone rang.

When I heard Mama's voice, I sat up and glanced at the clock. It was 9:15. Mama seldom called this late.

"What's happening?" I asked, folding myself into one corner of the couch and pulling my legs under me.

Mama started right in with her story, not stopping to take a breath. "Your cousin Rita was found murdered!"

"What happened?" I stuttered.

"What do you mean what happened? Somebody killed her!"

"How?"

"They burned her with fire!"

"They did what?"

"She was found inside her house, burned to death!"

"Maybe it was an accident," I said, remembering that only a few weeks before Mama's old Aunt Aggie had died. She too had been found burned to death in her own house.

"It was murder," Mama said. "They both were murdered."

"Take it easy," I said. "Calm down. You're getting too excited."

"Listen, Simone," Mama said. "A few weeks ago, Rita told me that she had run into a child who, she believed, was being sexually molested." She paused. "You did know that Rita was a caseworker?"

"Yes."

"Well, she said that she knew that a little girl who lived near Aunt Aggie was being sexually molested by her father."

"Who are these people?"

"The father is a Reverend Jones. He has a wife, a boy about sixteen, and a daughter about seven. Rita

10

believed that the man was having sex with his little girl!"

I touched the mute button on the television's remote control. "When did all this happen?" I asked.

Mama took a deep breath. "Let me backtrack," she said. "Rita told me that she stumbled upon the problem when she was visiting Aunt Aggie. Aunt Aggie had told Rita that the child's father, the so-called 'Reverend' Jones, bothered the child. Rita needed more proof than Aunt Aggie's story, but a few days later Aunt Aggie's house caught fire. Since Rita hadn't mentioned the story at the time, nobody thought much of it."

"Poor thing."

"You can't blame Rita," she said as if thinking out loud. "Aunt Aggie was ninety and she was always leaving things burning on the stove."

"What did Rita do after Miss Aggie died?"

"First she told me of her suspicion, and I suggested she start looking into the child's molestation again. I told her to talk to other neighbors, but nobody admitted knowing anything about the man bothering his daughter. Both Rita and I believed Aunt Aggie's story, and we were determined to prove that the man was bothering the child."

"Did Rita come up with some evidence?"

Mama's speech slowed. "That's why I'm calling you now, Simone," she said. "At about 2:45 last Monday morning, Hampton County fire fighters arrived at Rita's and found smoke coming from the house. Rita's body was inside. At first the fire fighters thought she died because of the fire, but wounds were found on her neck. Sheriff Abe called me a few minutes ago and told me that he had received the autopsy report and it showed that there was no carbon monoxide in Rita's lungs. She had been dead before the fire started."

"You mean somebody killed her?"

"Yes, Simone, and the terrible thing about it is that the poor woman didn't really have any evidence. She told me and a few other people that she had enough to put the child's father away for years, but she was lying. You know how Rita liked to exaggerate. Sheriff Abe thinks that maybe the old man set the house on fire to cover up the murder, but the fire smoldered for three to four hours and never really caught on."

"I can't believe somebody in Hampton would kill Rita."

"You calling me a liar?"

"No, Mama," I said. "It's just that in a small town like Hampton people don't kill each other."

"Simone, I expect better from you. In this day and time, no place is too small for a murder."

"I'm sorry," I said. "What do you want me to do?"

"I want you to come home this weekend. Rita didn't find evidence, but I will…. I must!"

"Mama," I said. "Both Aunt Aggie and Rita could have been wrong. The man might not have molested his child."

"That's beside the point now. Whether he's bothering the child or not, somebody killed Rita and set her house on fire, and I've got to find out who did it!"

My eyes wandered toward the pile of folders stacked against the wall. Mr. Jacoby had been in the middle of preparing a brief for trial when he remembered a statement by a hostile witness that suggested our client's alibi could be verified. He knew that the witness would deny the statement in court so he assigned me to dig through tons of papers to find the witness' exact words and then to trace the context of those words. With folders of reports, affidavits, transcripts, and depositions from several years of testimony, I thought it would take weeks before I could come up with something concrete. I frowned. "I don't think I can get home before the eighth of next month."

Mama cleared her throat. When she spoke, her voice was low. "Then I guess I'll have to start looking by myself."

I took a deep breath. "I'll be home in a few weeks."

"I can't wait that long!"

"Okay, I'll try to come home earlier, but please be careful," I said. "If the man is a murderer, he'd just as soon kill you."

Mama and I talked a few minutes longer. After I hung up the phone, I picked up a pencil and began turning it end over end. I felt a little sick inside. Rita had been near Mama's age, so she and I hadn't been that close, but she was Mama's cousin. I glanced at the folders. The prospect of finding a murderer was more exciting than plowing through a stack of folders looking for threads of conversation to prove an alibi. I sighed, walked over and picked up a handful of folders, and once again began my search.

That was eight months ago. Now Mama has fulfilled her moral obligation. And I'm going to set down for you, in chronological order, how she and I solved the murders of Aunt Aggie Nelson and Cousin Rita Ginn in South Carolina, but also how Mama helped clear a former college roommate of mine in Atlanta, Georgia, of the charge of committing murder.

13

Chapter 2

Saturday, July 8

"Who you looking for?" the woman asked, her eyes glaring at Mama and me.

The old black woman was hunchbacked, with thick lips and watery dark eyes that were cold and vacant. Her woolly gray hair looked as if it hadn't been combed in months. Her sunburned face had a little swelling in it, especially around her eyes, and there were fresh bruises on her cheeks. Despite the hot sun, she wore a brown cardigan sweater, unbuttoned, with a hole in the elbow, and she wore shoes she'd cut slits in for her corns. She smelled like something wet and rotten was seeping from her pores.

Mama was holding a stick in her hands that she'd been using to sift through the ashes. She smiled sweetly, her lively eyes meeting the woman's gaze directly. We were standing in the middle of the ash laden house that had been surrounded by spreading live oak trees whose branches met over the roadway. The house, before it had been reduced to ashes, had been occupied by my mama's Aunt Aggie Nelson.

Mama dropped the stick, pulled out a handkerchief, and patted her sweating face. When she spoke, her voice was soft, low, and ingratiating. "She was my aunt. I just had to come look at her old house one more time."

"I'm sorry," the old woman said, her head bowed. "Her house burned down and she was in it."

"I know," Mama said.

The woman sounded legitimately grief-stricken. "She's been dead a good while now." Her voice became hostile and her brow wrinkled. "Where you from?"

Mama kept smiling, her face gentle, sensitive. "Oh, I'm from Hampton," she said.

"She's been dead now about six weeks."

"Aunt Aggie used to do all my sewing for me...."

"She can't do no more sewing now," the woman interrupted. Her voice dropped as she stepped closer to the house. "She's dead and buried."

Mama sighed and stepped back beneath the spreading live oak tree whose branches offered shade. I watched and listened as I saw my mama's familiar sweetness.

"Her daughter Rita is dead too," she said.

"I ain't heard," the woman replied.

"A few days ago her own house burned down and she died. Two of them burned up in their own houses. That don't seem possible."

"Anything's possible," the woman answered, her eyes shifting toward the wooded area behind the house.

Mama eased back slowly. "It's strange that a house

15

would catch fire in this summer's heat. I don't reckon it could have been the heater."

The woman's eyes grew wide. All the while Mama was talking, my gaze was fixed on the woman's gnarled hands, clenched into fists, hands that appeared to have been broken and healed without medical attention. "What do I know," she said. "Fire started, burned everything down, Miss Aggie and all."

"Was Aunt Aggie a good neighbor?" Mama asked.

"I use to come up here and talk to her," the woman said, her manner relaxing slightly. She was a small woman, no more than five feet tall, with rounded shoulders. "She use to give me potato and tomato plants," she continued. "Sometimes she'd make me a frock. Now that she's gone, I guess there won't be any more new frocks."

Mama nodded and looked around.

The woman blinked, her mouth twisted into something that looked like a smile.

"Aunt Aggie did good things for lots of people," Mama said.

The woman's eyes seemed clouded. "Sometimes she made me a frock, sometimes she made me a cake or pie," she said.

Mama smiled. "You liked her...."

The woman's voice dropped. "She gave me things and made things for me and the child." When she said that, a little girl about eight years old appeared out of the tall grass from across the dusty road. She had large eyes that were sad; her whole face looked lonely and pathetic. Next to her stood a dog with pointed sticks for legs, a pointed face, one ear flopped and one straight.

"Mama, Daddy says come home," the child announced in an almost trembling voice.

The woman looked down at the child and sighed. "I'm coming," she said.

Suddenly, the air was very still, and I noticed that on each side of the road the woods stretched, obscuring from sight whatever house the child had come from. "But Daddy said...."

"I'm coming directly. Now get on back to the house!"

The little girl darted across the dusty dirt road, the dog following, but they both stood waiting for the old woman on the other side, standing in the tall grass.

"I've got to go," the woman said and quickly started across the road. In the middle of the road she stopped abruptly, her body stiffening. She looked back at Mama, and I could see her lips quivering even though her eyes were empty. When she spoke, her voice shook a little. "I reckon you'd better get out of here," she said. "Your Aunt Aggie is dead and gone.... Nobody can bring her back now."

Mama nodded and smiled. The woman turned and swiftly moved toward the child and the dog, which ran off a little ahead of her. Within seconds they had all disappeared through the narrow path between the trees. Mama's eyes were fixed on the trio, and I knew that her mind was registering the route the woman was taking. I felt myself shifting my weight from one foot to the other, but after a few seconds I joined Mama in digging through the rubble inside of the building. First, she inspected the door, then the floor, and finally what was left of the walls.

"What are you looking for?" I asked.

"I read a book not long ago," Mama said in almost a whisper. "It said that when you're searching for evidence of arson you need to look for certain patterns inside the building."

I stopped to look at her. "Can you identify an arson fire after reading one book?"

"I can look for specific things after reading one book," Mama answered.

I narrowed my eyes at her. "What would you do with the specific things if you find them?" I asked.

"I'll take it to Abe."

Hampton County's sheriff, Abe Stanley, had fallen under Mama's spell a few months after Daddy moved her into town. It happened when Mama was driving on that long stretch of road, Highway 601, that leads into Hampton from Estill and Nixville. Mama got a flat tire just about the time that Sheriff Abe drove by. Naturally, he stopped, and Mama hit him with a double barrel of her sweetness and charm, following up with baking him a sweet potato pie as a sign of gratitude. One pie led to another until Mama became a frequent visitor at the office. Between sweet potato pie and coffee, Mama, with little or no concrete evidence, helped Sheriff Abe nab several suspects in various crimes.

Sheriff Abe learned to respect Mama's intuition, and he liked talking to her since it usually ended up with him putting somebody behind bars as well as getting himself some more tender morsels of sweet potato pie. Daddy wasn't impressed. He didn't like Mama playing detective, but he accepted it as the price for keeping Mama happy in Hampton, South Carolina.

"What will Sheriff Abe do with your so-called 'evidence?'" I asked, staring at Mama, who continued to probe the ashes. "This is Jasper County and you don't have Jasper County's sheriff in your pocket."

Mama stopped abruptly. Still on her hands and knees, she ordered, "Go to the car and bring me that box of Ziploc bags I got in the backseat!"

I obeyed. I knew by her tone that she had found something important. Mama took the bags. In one she put some ash and other debris. In a second one, she put samples of burned, charred dirt. In a third, she put samples of unburned dirt. I watched her, thinking of Aunt Aggie, a poor old woman who had died so tragically. A welcome breeze stirred, and a dog barked in the distance.

"Abe has got to look into this thing,"

"You're probably right," I said.

Mama walked out beyond the perimeter of the burned building, stopped, and turned around. She raised an eyebrow. "Now we can start looking for what started the fire."

The sun glowed orange through the tops of the pine trees. We stepped back out of the brilliant sunshine heat and moved into the tall grass, plundering through the weeds, crawling around slowly on our hands and knees. It had been six weeks since the house had burned, six weeks of summer rains and rapid growth, but Mama's hunch was strong. She was sure she could find whatever was used to set the house ablaze.

Periodically, I straightened up, trying to keep the crick out of my back. "The Jasper County sheriff probably found whatever evidence there was," I said.

Mama looked up at me. "He wasn't looking for anything, so why would he examine or move anything. Remember, we're talking about an old woman…. Aunt

Aggie was at least ninety. I got a feeling that the sheriff figured it was bound to happen sooner or later."

I heard the dog bark again, loud enough to make me uncomfortable. "We're being watched," I said.

Mama's eyes were toward the charred earth. "I don't think so," she said without looking up. "Even if we are, I'm not leaving here until I find out what started the fire."

"I hope we can find something that will stand up in a court of law," I said, my mind wandering toward the legal aspects of Mama's conclusions.

"You know there are experts who can dig through these kind of ruins, perform laboratory tests, and can tell conclusively if arson occurred."

The dog barked again.

"Mama," I said, "I do believe that somebody is watching us!"

"So?"

"It could be the same person you think set Miss Aggie's house on fire."

"I ain't scared. I can't imagine anybody that's low enough to set a ninety-year-old woman's house on fire in the middle of the night being any match for the two of us."

We heard something rustle, and I jumped as an old cat streaked past us. Mama laughed softly but I swore under my breath. We kept moving on our hands and knees, pushing back the thick growth, going deeper, following Mama's hunch. Mosquitoes, gnats, and yellow jackets hovered over us, every once in a while one tasting tiny samples of my blood. "What are we looking for again?" I asked.

"Look!" Mama said, pointing into the weeds, at

about the same time I asked my question.

"What?" I asked, slapping my already tender arm as I tried to keep mosquitoes and gnats from overdosing on my blood.

Mama reached into a boggy undergrowth and pulled at a weathered old can covered with caked-on dirt that had lodged under a clump of overgrown weeds. The smell of damp rotting vegetation permeated the atmosphere, but Mama pulled at the can until she finally released it.

"What in the world is that dirty thing?" I asked.

"A can," Mama whispered. "An old kerosene can and some rags."

Something rustled again. "What was that?"

"Probably that same old cat," Mama said.

"Well, Miss Marple," I said sarcastically, "now that you've got the old can, let's try to find our way out of here." Mama's glinting eyes suddenly began staring, her face frozen, her body tensed. It took me a few seconds to focus my attention on the sound that had startled her. It was a short, rattling sound.

"Don't move," Mama said, her voice tight. "There's a rattler over there."

The sound was clear and distinct, and we both concentrated on trying to determine which direction it was coming from. We saw the snake at about the same time. It was coiled, warning us not to make a move in its direction.

A breeze stirred again as Mama and I kneeled there, in the thick brush, for what seemed like hours, neither moving or speaking. Finally, the sound died down, the snake uncoiling and moving past us, satisfied that we were getting its message.

21

When it was well out of sight, Mama brushed her cheek with one hand and with the other she gripped the small kerosene can and whispered, "Move back slowly. Try to move back the same way we came in."

We crawled backward in silence, cautiously trying to listen to every sound. When we were back into the clearing, I made a face of thankfulness. We both stood for a moment, collecting ourselves. Then I started walking toward the car.

Mama's breathing was calm, her head tilted like a bird staring at a worm. She had wiped her sooty hands on a tissue she'd taken from her purse. Now she stood looking at the dirty old kerosene can. Suddenly, her chin came up. "Tomorrow when you go back to Atlanta," she said, her voice steady, "I'll come back to Ridgeland…. I need to talk to my source again."

Chapter 3

Sunday, July 9

On Sunday morning I woke early, stretching my arms and legs. I was covered with insect bites; my flesh was stinging with inch-sized welts. I got up and went to the bathroom, reaching into the medicine cabinet for something to ease my discomfort. A few minutes later, I smelled the coffee and bacon coming from the kitchen. Whatever pain Mama caused me, she always made up for it when she cooked. Her grits, scrambled eggs, bacon, biscuits, and coffee made me forget about the flies, gnats, and mosquitoes, although nothing could make me forget about the snake. After slathering on calamine lotion, I walked into the kitchen.

"Good morning," Mama said.

"Good morning," I replied, walking out onto the back porch and tasting the early morning air. It was still a little cool, my favorite time of the day in South

Carolina. It seemed as if time stopped, stood still, and rested a minute. Just before sunrise when the sky began to lighten, showing dark, early clouds, there was a pause when nothing moved, not even time. It made me happy to be there at that moment, and I tried to stand perfectly still, to be immobile with the old man who carried the hourglass. Fifteen minutes later the moment had vanished, with the daylight flashing from the east. I stepped back into the kitchen and walked over to the stove to pour myself a cup of coffee. Daddy was sitting at the breakfast table.

"What time are you leaving for Atlanta?" Mama asked.

I took a slow sip of the hot liquid. "I guess I'll leave as soon as I've eaten," I said.

Daddy looked up. "Why are you going back so early?" he asked. He wore his bathrobe wide open, showing his hairy legs and plaid boxer shorts. There are things about my father that have always been a bit of a mystery to me. The way he does certain things seem to defy logic. For example, he would always wear his bathrobe opened so his legs and boxer shorts were exposed.

"Why wear the bathrobe at all?" I once asked.

"It's proper," he answered.

This morning I smiled, thinking of his contradictory nature. "My new case is special," I answered. "The client is Cheryl LaFlamme, who was my roommate for a time at college."

Mama didn't seem to have heard me. She was pouring Daddy's coffee. When she finished, she put a platter of bacon and eggs on the table to join the bowl of grits, sliced cantaloupe, and a pitcher of orange juice.

Then she wiped her hands on her apron.

For a moment, I forgot about the bites and straightened up in my chair.

"Did you fix biscuits?" Daddy asked.

"Give me a minute," she said. She opened the oven, reached in, got the pan of biscuits, and dropped it on the stove top. She picked it up again and dropped it so the biscuits would break away from the pan bottom. Mama piled them on the plate and set them on the table.

"Where's the honey?" Daddy asked.

Mama looked at him with a steady gaze. "In the cabinet," she said. It was her signal to Daddy that she had served him as much as she was going to.

Daddy smiled. The look in his eyes told me that even in the kitchen, in her house dress, Mama's soft skin, mouth, and eyes held him captive. He got up, bathrobe wide open, and plundered through some condiments that Mama kept in a kitchen cabinet. When he found the honey, he sat back down, picked up a hot biscuit, and stuck his finger in to form a cavity in which he poured honey. He took a bite, nodded his head, licked honey off his hand, and smiled. He leaned back in his chair and relaxed his shoulders. "Candi, you've outdone yourself again," he said, his mouth full of bread.

Mama smiled and nodded. I'd already fixed my plate, so I took a bite of eggs, a bite of grits, and two bites of bacon.

"What were you saying about your college roommate?" Mama asked.

I smiled. "I thought that had gotten by you," I said. "Mr. Jacoby is representing Cheryl LaFlamme. She and I shared a small apartment my first year of college."

Mama nodded but said nothing. I suspected that she

25

was thinking about how she was going to prove that Reverend Jones had murdered her aunt and her cousin. I was thinking about the young woman with whom I had shared six months of my life in a small kitchenette apartment near Emory University. Two things I remembered about Cheryl: she was lonely, and she bathed constantly. I don't know if it bothered me more that she was being charged with murder or that she was motivated by something so elusive as a damaged psyche.

After breakfast Daddy had to check my Honda to be satisfied that it could make the four-hour trip.

"Is it all right?" I asked as I threw my overnight bag into the backseat of the car. Even though my daddy was a bulky, broad-shouldered man who wore middle-age well, I could see that his hair was a little grayer.

"It looks pretty good," Daddy answered. "You've been taking good care of it."

I smiled. "To be honest, somebody else gets to take the credit. He's a good mechanic."

Daddy stared thoughtfully. "You're trying to tell me that there's somebody in your life that's going to replace your daddy?" he asked.

"Nobody can ever take your place, Daddy," I teased, leaning over and kissing him on his cheek. "But there is a certain somebody. Don't worry. I'll let you know if it becomes serious."

Daddy asked no questions because, unlike Mama, he assumed that whatever information you wanted him to know you'd volunteer. My father was not curious.

When I went back into the kitchen, Mama was quietly finishing up the dishes. She walked over to the counter, wiped it, then moved toward the stove.

"What are you going to do with the gas can you

found at Aunt Aggie's house?" I asked, going to the refrigerator and getting a glass of orange juice, then sitting down at the table.

"I'm going back to Ridgeland. I want to talk to several people."

"What do you hope to find out?"

"I want to know more about Reverend Jones…, what kind of church he preaches in. I can't imagine a preacher letting his wife and child go to church without decent clothes. I don't think he is a preacher."

"After that," I repeated, "what are you going to do with the stuff you picked up at Aunt Aggie's house?"

"I guess I'll stop by to see Sheriff Abe tomorrow morning on my way to work. Leave it with him and see if he can make use of it."

I sipped the juice and swallowed.

She looked around approvingly at her spotless kitchen.

"Mama, be careful. You know, I really don't think it's a good idea for you to go snooping around old burned out houses alone," I said.

"I need to examine Rita's house."

"You're going to crawl around her house and run up on another snake too."

Mama walked across the kitchen to the window. The bright sun was beaming through the white curtains. "I've got to," she said, staring out into the morning light. "But not alone," she added quickly. "I'll wait until you come back next Saturday."

"I can't come back next week," I said.

"What has this Cheryl done?"

"She is *accused*," I said, with emphasis on the word 'accused,' "of killing a man," I said.

"Did she kill him?"

"She shot him three times in the back," I said.

Mama frowned. "That's your problem.... My problem is proving that Reverend Jones killed Aunt Aggie and Cousin Rita."

"Mama," I said. "Please don't go crawling through that house alone."

She paused and nodded. "Maybe you're right. I'll ask Sheriff Abe to get one of his deputies to do it for me."

"Thank goodness," I said, taking a deep breath. I rose, put my empty glass in the sink, then walked over and put my arms around her neck. "I'd really feel better if you did," I told her. She moved slightly. "Besides, he'll probably know better what to look for since he's probably read two books to your one."

We laughed. Mama raised her eyebrows. "When will you be back home?" she asked, her voice reserved yet calm.

I moved away and scratched my arms. "In a couple of weeks."

She looked down at my welted arms. "You all right?" she asked.

I nodded perfunctorily, thinking how Cliff, the guy I'd been dating for almost six months, would laugh when I told him about how my mother and I were down on our hands and knees crawling through the underbrush when we met an assertive rattlesnake.

When I looked at Mama, I could see the curiosity in her face. I shook myself free of my thoughts.

"After I find out what church this Reverend Jones preaches in, I'm going to try to find some of his church members and talk to them. I want you to go with me," she said. "If nothing else, maybe they can give us some idea of what kind of man the preacher is."

That sounded safe enough, I thought. "You get names and addresses, and when I come back, we'll go together to talk with them."

It was noon when I drove away from my parents' house. The sky was brilliant. I looked forward to the trip alone. The warmth and light streamed on the road that took me into Augusta and on to Atlanta. For forty-five minutes, my mind shifted between the music on the cassette that I had put in the tape deck and Mama's case. Finally, I drove into an Exxon station in a small town. A young boy sat on a wooden chair reading an old magazine. I pumped gas, paid the boy, and drove away.

The town consisted of a general store, a convenience store, a town hall, and a small post office. It had sprawling side streets, small houses, and mobile homes. A total contrast to Atlanta, I thought. Then my mind shifted from Mama's mystery to the new assignment that Mr. Jacoby had handed me Friday afternoon around four o'clock. I had barely begun reading when I realized that I had known the client, had actually slept in the same room with her. After that, the case took on a new meaning.

By the time I arrived in Atlanta, I had worked up an appetite for reviewing Cheryl's story. As soon as I could sit down, I pulled the manila folder from my briefcase and began reading.

According to Mr. Jacoby's notes, the murder victim was a man named Harold Young, and his sister was both wealthy and influential. She was using her contacts to pressure the district attorney to rush the trial and demand the death penalty for our client. Mr. Jacoby wanted to maneuver the situation in our client's favor by introducing evidence to prove mitigating circumstances for the shooting of Young.

My friend Cheryl was a white woman about my age. Her statement was that she had decided to take a vacation to the Bahamas on the advice of her psychiatrist, Dr. Joyce. She and her friend Penny boarded a plane in Atlanta to fly to Miami, where they were to get on a cruise ship. She saw Harold Young for the first time on the plane and, for some reason, she believed that she had seen him before.

Harold Young was with his wife, a petite woman whose pasty complexion begged for some sun. Ironically, it turned out that Harold Young and his wife were booked on the same cruise ship. Mr. Young was ill most of the trip, so Cheryl spent a great deal of time with Mrs. Young. From Mrs. Young, Cheryl learned of where Young lived and worked. When she returned to Atlanta, she stalked him for months. Finally, her feelings overwhelming, she wanted to confront him. "I had to talk to him," she had said. "I had no choice.... I had to tell him what I was feeling."

Apparently, she had killed the man. She had walked into Young's office and shot him in the back. Mr. Jacoby's defense was that, as she stalked Young, bits and pieces of memory began unfolding in her mind. By the time she arrived at J. Higgins & Sons the day of the shooting, she wanted to confront Young and expose him. She brought the gun, she said, to use it to force him to confess what he had done to her. When she walked into his office, he was sitting at his desk, his back toward her. She shut the door and, for a brief moment, she simply stood and stared at him.

All the while, Cheryl said, a monster was growing inside of her as mental images exploded in her head. Horrible memories came down like a flood. She accused Young. He sat quietly, ignoring her. She pulled out the gun and demanded that he confess what he had done to her. He continued to sit with his back to her, saying nothing the entire time. She spoke again; he ignored her. She began shooting him in the back...a total of three shots.

Despite Cheryl's dramatic account of the motive for the shooting, the fact that she had the gun with her and had purchased it several days before was reason enough *not* to believe that she had acted on impulse. She wanted to force him into admitting his guilt, something she felt she could do with a gun. There was no use working up an alibi, there were five witnesses who saw Cheryl go into Young's office minutes before the shooting. And, when the police arrived, she was standing in Young's office holding the weapon that killed him.

I thought of how frightened Cheryl must be right now. She hadn't many friends. When I had known her, she had been totally immersed in getting an education. I sighed. Poor girl, I thought. Her life hinged on motive, a motive I was beginning to feel obligated to prove.

I was accustomed to deciphering Mr. Jacoby's handwriting, so I read with interest that he had already done some of the legwork and had talked with Cheryl's psychiatrist, Dr. Joyce, a woman who had been treating her. Dr. Joyce believed that Cheryl was suffering from some kind of traumatic experience that had happened to her when she was a little girl, and it was possible that, when she accidentally ran across Young, memories began to be dredged up that had been buried deep within her subconscious, memories of having been molested by him as a child. And, according to the doctor, it was possible that the memories had pressured her into attempting to rectify what had been done to her as a helpless child.

Mr. Jacoby's note admitted that he was fishing but he wanted me to find out whether or not the sexual molestation happened, or at least if there was a possibility that it had occurred.

I remembered sharing a room with Cheryl, remembered how she never had friends, how she never talked to her parents, how she took three or four baths a day.

I put down the manila folder. This doesn't make sense, I thought. How can something buried deep within the subconscious twenty-five years earlier turn a warm and sensitive woman into a cold-blooded murderer. I swallowed. Mama would probably call this case, "Murder by the Subconscious."

I shook my head. Forget about Mama, I thought. She's in South Carolina crawling around burned out houses and looking for the good Reverend Jones. It was my job, my duty to find the connection between the dead man and Cheryl.

I flipped through the pages of the folders again. In large letters, Mr. Jacoby had written, *"Cheryl LaFlamme was adopted when she was seven."* I frowned. Records prior to her adoption would have been permanently closed, I thought.

I'm accustomed to digging through public records, so I tried thinking of places to begin my search. I went over everything again in my mind, probing, testing, searching for flaws. I could find none. I tried to put myself in her place. The Cheryl I had known had been a shy, quiet woman.

"She'll be convicted!" I whispered. "Unless I can dig something up, she'll get the chair!"

Chapter 4

Friday, July 14

I had been back in Atlanta a week before I had a chance to see Cliff Roberts, the guy I had been dating for six months. He had been out of town most of the week, calling and leaving messages, but we hadn't had a chance to talk. The last message he had left on my answering machine was that he would be over tonight, around 8:00. I looked at the clock on the wall. It was 7:30, and I was hungry.

After a week of trying to dig up my client's past, I hadn't come up with anything. I had exhausted the usual channel of working through court and school records. Now I was down to examining, in minute details, the transcripts of our client's hypnotized recollections of her so-called "sexual abuse." It was tedious and at times confusing.

I longed to talk about the situation, to get a fresh

prospective, but the other paralegal in the office refused to discuss individual cases. And she had given me no explanation for her refusal. She had merely given me a flat "no" when I had asked. I was in the habit of talking things over with Mama.

I had just about decided to talk the case over with Mama anyway. I knew she would have ideas. Despite the fact that I earned a very good living digging up details that helped put certain individuals securely away in prison, I knew that my mama would be the one source to set me in the right direction. I was mulling over how I was going to talk her into helping me when Cliff rang the doorbell.

Cliff, a good looking tall guy, wearing green casual slacks and a dark silk shirt, pulled me into his arms and kissed me. "Well, young lady," he said when he finally let go, "it's good to have you back."

"It's good to have *you* back," I said, moving away in an effort to catch my breath. Cliff looked good to me, and seeing him now, completely at ease, made me think of my father. He was easygoing like my father, but he had a slightly tough edge underneath that I'd only glimpsed briefly. He was a multifaceted man, good with his hands.

Cliff was a lawyer, recently having passed the bar. His expertise was domestic law, and he had gotten a job with a firm of divorce lawyers. He had a future, but I still wasn't sure about him. I worked with lawyers every day, and I knew that most of them had a ruthless, searing temper that showed itself whenever they dealt with trouble, grief, or vicious people day after day. I wondered whether the pressure of his profession would eventually overwhelm him, bringing out the cold and hard nature that I'd observed with some of the lawyers in our office.

I didn't want to find out too late that Cliff wasn't the kind of man that my father was. I remember thinking, when I was about ten years old, that for all my mother's charm and intelligence, my father was the most important person in her life, and I wanted the same kind of man.

"What's for supper?" Cliff said, looking around the room, and easing down onto the leather sofa.

"I'll tell you when I see a menu." I turned and walked into the bathroom.

"You know, Simone," he said, raising his voice a little louder, "I really like this room. It has soft edges like you. And I like its scent!"

I walked out and stood in the bathroom door. "You'll like the odor of a restaurant just as well."

"I bet it wouldn't be as lovely as this room, with its cream and rose colors, its lace curtains, its leather sofa."

"But there's food there and there's none here.... There's absolutely nothing here to eat."

He smiled sensuously. "We could send out."

I picked up my purse and walked toward the front door. "Better still, we could go out, get something to eat, and then come back to the apartment."

Cliff begged. "Please."

"Nope. Tonight you're going to buy me a meal, something you've neglected to do for the past few weeks. Anyway, I got a case I want to talk to you about. It'll probably be easier to talk in a restaurant."

His voice was soft. "Listen, Simone, let's *not* talk shop tonight, please. I've been knee-deep in a legal mess that has taken me into three states just this week alone, and heaven knows how much more traveling it's going to take. What some people will do in a divorce is unbelievable. Anyway, if you want to do something physical, like arm wrestle," he smiled, "I'm with you, but please, no shoptalk tonight."

"In that case," I said, turning the deadbolt, "instead of coming back to the apartment after dinner, we'll go straight to the gym."

The next morning Cliff got up early and went downstairs to wash and wax both our cars. I got up early and made coffee and toast. I'd never caught on to the way Mama cooked large breakfasts.

At 10:15, Cliff hadn't returned, so I decided to get out of the house. My car was in the apartment parking lot but Cliff's BMW was nowhere in sight. I decided against driving and walked the few blocks to take the MARTA into downtown. I mulled around picking up odds and ends from one store after another and ended up at the Mall.

It was around four o'clock when I got back to the apartment. Cliff was applying elbow grease in waxing my car. There was one message on the answering machine. Donna, my best friend, had called. I went to the bathroom, then came back to the living room, dropped down on the sofa, and returned her phone call.

"Listen," Donna said, "I need your help."

"What's up?"

"Ernest has got this friend...."

"Donna, you know that Cliff and I...."

"I'm not asking you to sleep with the guy. I just want you to go out with us—Ernest, me, and the guy—for a meal; that's all."

"You know that Cliff and I are...."

"I know that you and Cliff are like me and Ernest, but I'm not trying to come between that. I'm just asking you to go out for a meal, that's all."

"I don't think I should."

"Why not?"

"If the shoe was on the other foot, would you do it for me?"

"Sure, I would. You know that."

"I don't know that. Anyway, I don't think Cliff would like it."

"Why not? Remember, he owes you one."

I stared thoughtfully for a moment. "What do you mean?"

"Remember about three months ago when his colleague's sister came to town and he took her out for drinks? You remember, he broke a date with you. Said it was business, you remember?"

I had forgotten but suddenly the memories flooded my mind. I sighed. "I remember."

"You and I talked about it for hours. He wasn't going to see the girl again; it was a favor, a favor to a colleague not a favor to a friend, like I am."

"You're not being fair."

"Ask him," Donna insisted. "Tell him that the guy is a friend of Ernest's, in town for tonight. That's all; tomorrow morning 8:00 A.M., he's out of here, I swear."

"I hate you doing this to me, Donna."

"Listen, we're friends. When you need me, I'm here for you, aren't I? And when things don't go right with you and Cliff, who do you call?"

"You're hitting below the belt."

"I need this favor, Simone. Honestly, just this once."

"Why is it that I don't believe you, Donna?"

"I promised Ernest that you'll go out with us. Please say yes."

"Let me talk it over with Cliff."

"Call me back right away."

"As soon as I talk it over with him, I'll call."

"Simone, remember we're friends. We've been friends through three of your boyfriends and four of mine. What we've got, I mean our relationship, outlasts boyfriends, remember that."

She had a point. "Thanks for reminding me."

I hung up the phone and went downstairs, where Cliff was still polishing what was left of the chrome on his BMW.

"What's your plans for tonight?" I asked, trying to keep my voice even.

"Ain't got none," he said without looking up. "What do you want to do?"

"Donna called me and she asked me a favor."

"What?"

I tried to choose my words carefully. "You know her boyfriend Ernest; well, he has got a friend in town, just overnight, and they want me to accompany them to dinner."

Cliff stopped rubbing and looked up. He had never looked more handsome, with his cocoa brown skin, dark eyes, and short Afro haircut. "You want to go?" he asked, his voice low.

"Not if you want me to do something with you," I said gently.

His voice was calm. "I can go work out at the gym." He began rubbing the chrome on his car again. "Why don't you go out with them? I really want to work out.

I need to work my body." He smiled. "I'll grab some kind of take-out order and come back and wait for you upstairs."

I waited a moment while what he said raced through my mind. "You mean you'll wait for me in my apartment?"

He nodded. "Why not?"

I frowned. "No! If I go, then you can't stay in my apartment."

"Why?"

"I don't want you to. It's like you waiting to see what time I get home. My father never did that, and I won't...."

"Okay, you go out with Donna and Ernest, I'll pick up a take-out order, and you can come to *my* apartment tomorrow morning for breakfast."

"You really don't mind?"

Cliff looked up again, his brow lifted. "Yes, I mind," he said, his lips a little curved. "But this divorce case I'm working on is an eye opener. All this stuff could be avoided if the parties involved just trusted each other, that's all. They're about to destroy each other and their children because they don't trust. I don't want that in our relationship. I trust you, and...." He reached up and pecked me on the lips. "...I want you to trust me, Simone. It's the only way I want this thing to work."

I felt a surge of optimism. I reached down and kissed him tenderly. "You're pretty neat," I said, thinking that this relationship might work after all.

"You are too. Now you'd better go before I change my mind," he said, turning back to rub the poor chrome. I turned, went back upstairs, and called Donna.

"What time are you going to pick me up?" I asked.

"Around 8:00 P.M."

"What should I wear?"

"Something sexy."

"No way."

"I'm only kidding, girlfriend; wear something comfortable. I tell you, all we're going to do is go to dinner, something Italian, I think. Ernest said the guy wants to see the Underground, so we'll go downtown and probably end up in Ernest's favorite bar for drinks. The main thing is to wear comfortable shoes."

"Okay," I said, about to hang up the phone. "And, oh Donna…," I added.

"Yeah."

"Don't do this again. The next time the answer *will* be no."

"I got you," she said and hung up the phone.

Sunday night, after I got back to my apartment, the telephone rang. It was Mama.

"Listen, do me a favor and research something for me at your library," she said.

"Okay, what?"

"I want you to find out what kind of a man molests a young child…. I mean, what is his personality, his background, his history, that sort of stuff?"

For a few moments, I was speechless. That's it, I thought, remembering my client. Mama hit the nail on the head. If I can't find Cheryl's history, I could search Harold Young's history. I laughed.

"What's the matter?"

"I'm investigating the wrong person."

"What do you mean?"

"I'll tell you later. What did you have in mind about

41

your case?"

"Well, I was thinking, if this Reverend Jones is a child molester and ultimately an arsonist and we can go back into his past, we might be able to dig up the kind of evidence that we need to support what we believe to be true about him. It will strengthen the child abuse case."

"You're right! And, to show you how much I agree with you, as soon as I get the information, I'll bring it to you."

"But," Mama said, a bit of surprise in her tone, "you told me that Mr. Jacoby wanted you to stay in Atlanta. You can mail the material to me."

"I've changed my mind. I'll research the molester's profile and bring the information home for your case. Anything else you want me to do for you on this end?"

"What?" Mama asked.

"Anything else you want me to look up? Information about arson, anything like that?"

"No."

"Well, as soon as I get the information together, I'll bring it home. Maybe next week, I'm not sure. But certainly the weekend after that."

"Okay."

"And, Mama," I added, "you are a very wise and intelligent woman."

"I know," Mama said, just before she put the receiver down.

Chapter 5

It worked out that I couldn't get home until the weekend, but that didn't mean that things didn't start happening the moment I talked to Mama. The very next morning I began checking court records and the credit bureaus. Oddly, there wasn't much to learn about Harold Young. After he had graduated from college in New York, he moved to Atlanta to work for J. Higgins & Sons clothiers.

He hadn't been affiliated with any organization, religious or otherwise. Judging from the paper trail that I dug up, Harold Young appeared to have been an upper-middle-class businessman whose life, by my standards, had been very dull. His life revolved around his work and his home.

I decided my next move would be to talk to people who had known Harold Young, something that wasn't easy. His doctor's receptionist, (his doctor refused to talk to me personally) said that there wasn't anything out of the ordinary about him. He was nice and easy-going. She said he was an inconspicuous man who blended into his environment almost unnoticed. It seemed, from what I had gathered up to this point, that Harold Young's only social contacts had been his wife and his sister.

I called the receptionist at J. Higgins & Sons trying to get to talk to somebody there, but she gave me the runaround. I never really got to talk to anybody. Finally, out of desperation, I took a long shot and called Young's wife to ask for an appointment. Maybe I could learn something about the dead man's past.

To be honest, I didn't think she would see me. After all, it was my boss who was defending her husband's murder. Still, I felt that it was strange that it was her husband's sister who was pushing for a speedy prosecution rather than Mrs. Young. It was a long shot, but I was desperate to talk to somebody to try to learn what kind of man Harold Young might have been. Or rather, whether he was the kind of man who would have molested a five-year-old child. Surprisingly, she agreed to see me on Friday two weeks away.

It wasn't much but it was the only opening I had. I met with Mr. Jacoby and told him my idea. He sat smiling, making steeples with his hands. I don't think he had any particular personal feelings for Cheryl, but I sensed that he was glad that she had been my friend.

He cleared his throat with a skeptical hum.

"The prosecutor is pushing for an early trial."

"Get as much time as you can," I said.

"You think she killed him deliberately?" he asked.

"I can't think anymore," I said. "But I believe that the Cheryl I shared space with for six months is incapable of killing anyone."

He smiled. "She was driven," he said.

"If I can prove that, it'll save her from the death penalty," I said.

He nodded. "I'll push for a postponement. Find me something!"

I mentioned Mama's uncanny ability to get to the bottom of mysteries.

He smiled, leaned forward, and opened his hands. "You want me to meet her?" he asked.

I nodded. "It's a long shot, but it's the only shot I've got for an old friend," I said.

Mr. Jacoby laughed. "I like the way you feel about this one," he said. "It gives you dimension."

"Dimension my foot," I said, standing and walking toward his door. "It gives me sleepless nights."

I spent the next few days researching to get an idea of the profiles of a child molester and an arsonist. What I found was interesting, and I jotted down several personality traits to check out about our murder victim. I also used the time to mentally map out my strategy of trying to look backwards in the history of the man our client had killed.

Now that Mama had put me on the right track to find what I could about Harold Young, something began nudging me to get her involved in the case. Looking back, I know now that it was the reason I had mentioned her to Mr. Jacoby. Anyway, by the time I was driving to Hampton, I'd already decided that my trip would be to accomplish two things. First, I would go with Mama to visit Reverend Jones' church members, listen to her, and try to learn how to ask the right questions to get the right answers. And second, I would ask her to come up to Atlanta and go with me when I visited Mrs. Young.

There was no use fooling myself; only Mama could get the woman to tell her things about her husband that I needed to know—things that would help me get a fix on whether our client and Harold Young had ever been together. I needed my mama's expertise and I wasn't about to blow this chance to find the one thread that I needed to unravel my mystery. I still wondered whether my work would do any good. Our client was going to jail for murder; there was no doubt about that. But now I was excited. Mama and I would be working together, both in Atlanta and Hampton.

On this summer's morning, the sun was just coming up when I drove from Atlanta and began the four-hour drive to Hampton. I was in the mood for low and mellow music, so that's the kind of tape I slipped into the tape deck before I pulled out of the apartment building's parking lot. I wanted to be able to think, with as little distraction as possible, about how I was going to ask for Mama's help with my case. I wanted her to take a couple days off from her job and come to Atlanta to work with me. I smiled, thinking of my mama as a big city detective. I had the feeling that Mama had expected that this would happen: she had waited me out, knowing that I would have to come to her.

It was twelve o'clock when I drove up in our front yard. (I say 'our' yard, but in truth I'd never lived in Hampton. My parents didn't move there until after their three children—my brothers and I—were grown and out on our own. My brothers, both of whom live in

Jacksonville, Florida, are married with two children each, and both their wives hate Hampton. So, despite the fact that the trip takes them about the same four hours as it takes me from Atlanta, they don't make the trip as often as I do.

At one time, my brothers tried to camouflage the fact that their wives didn't like visiting Hampton by saying that the reason I had to make the trip so often was because I let Mama pull me into her "private eye" games.

When I walked into the house, my father was eating. Mama had laid out a spread for him—fried chicken, fried okra, tomatoes, string beans, corn, rice, and corn bread, with both apple and sweet potato pie cooling on top of the stove.

"Why are you eating such a heavy meal in the middle of the day?"

"I don't know what time we're going to get home," Mama said. "And I'm not cooking anymore today or tomorrow."

"Sit down and eat," Daddy said, pointing to the chair next to him. I obeyed, since I never tried resisting Mama's cooking.

It was another hour and a half before Mama and I pulled out of the yard and headed down Highway 601 toward Savannah.

I took out my notebook. "Which one of Reverend Jones' church members are we going to visit first?"

"Reverend Jones ain't got a church," Mama said.

"But I thought you said we were going to visit his church members."

"I found out that Reverend Jones doesn't have a church or any church members. What I found out is that a long time ago, maybe ten, twelve years, the man had a little church with a few old ladies, but they all died and he never bothered dropping the title 'Reverend.' He doesn't profess any religious denomination."

"So where are we heading?"

"You remember that woman we met at Aunt Aggie's house?"

I nodded.

"Well, that's the Reverend Jones' wife. She's got a cousin in Tarboro, and she's agreed to talk to me this afternoon. We're visiting a Miss Barbara Flemming."

"And what do we do after that?"

"We find some place nice and quiet and you tell me what's on your mind."

I fought back a laugh. "I should have known you'd already figured out I want to talk to you about something."

Mama blinked a few times. "It was no big feat. When I called you and asked you to do some research for me, *something* I said caused you to get all excited. I want to know what it was I said and find out if it has helped you."

"Okay," I said holding up my hand. "I admit it: I need your expertise."

"We'll talk about it after we make this visit."

"What progress have you made on your case?"

"Sheriff Abe had one of his deputies examine Rita's house, and the deputy did find evidence of arson, so at least that fire has been opened as an official murder case. The sheriff of Jasper County is following up on information Sheriff Abe gave him." Mama winked. "Unfortunately, they couldn't find that kind of evidence

48

at Aunt Aggie's house; it was just too long after the fire and weather has destroyed any hopes of proving beyond a doubt that her house was set on fire. Right now the sheriff is working with the Jasper County Sheriff's Department in trying to dig up information on the Reverend Jones."

"Wait a minute. You got all that done since I was home a little over two weeks ago?"

Mama nodded. "It was obvious to me the day I talked to that old woman that she'd been beaten, probably by that boy and that so-called 'husband' of hers. I had a local caseworker talk to her, but she denies being mistreated. She even refuses to leave the man, and the law can't make her do it."

"What can you do about it?"

"I don't know yet; that's why I'm going to see her family."

Mama's light blue Ford turned into a yard straight from a dirt road and stopped in front of a wooden house that looked like something out of *Uncle Tom's Cabin*. The house was of unpainted board and batten, bleached and rotted by the elements. An old woman sat in a rocking chair on the porch. We stepped up on two cinder blocks to get off the ground and onto the porch.

"How you doing today?" Mama asked.

The woman had mango colored skin, no teeth, and deep large eyes that set back in her forehead. She reminded me of a raccoon. "I'm doing fine," she answered.

"I reckon you've been expecting me," Mama said in the colloquial dialect she often used when she wanted to give the impression she had been born and raised in the area.

"You the woman from Hampton who was supposed to come see me?" the old woman replied.

"The very one," Mama said, smiling sweetly. "If I may, I'd like to ask you about your cousin who's married to the Reverend Jones down behind Ridgeland."

"You mean Sister-gal?" the old woman said, as she slapped at the flies surrounding a half-empty plate of what looked like rice and brown gravy. "I'm her mama's sister."

Mama laughed. "So you're not her cousin. I declare, I must have gotten some misinformation."

"I don't know about information, but I'm Sister-gal's mama's sister. I was in the house the very day that Sister-gal was born."

"When was the last time you saw Sister-gal?"

"Shucks, I ain't seen Sister-gal since before her last child was born. Must been eight, nine years ago."

"She ain't been to see you?"

"Sister-gal? Her old man stopped her from coming to visit her people long before he said that the Lord had called him to preach."

"Might be a good idea if you visited her."

"Visit her!" the old woman laughed scornfully. "I'm her auntie, ain't I? Sister-gal should be coming here to take care of me in my old age."

It was clear that the old woman didn't like the idea of visiting her niece, so Mama wisely changed the subject. "You think her old man is touched in the head?" she asked, pointing a finger toward her own forehead.

"That boy is right pitiful," the woman said, shaking her head. "I've known him since he was born."

"You know his people?"

She shook her head. "They use to live right down

50

the road a piece. Did you know that his mama was his pa's daughter?"

Mama's voice dropped to a whisper. "You mean the old man fathered the boy by his own daughter?" Mama asked.

The old woman nodded. "It's a fact. It was a shame the way he aggravated that poor girl. They found her dead, you know, and the child was only a few months old. The old man and his wife raised the boy, never gave him no schooling. No matter, the blood was too thick, the boy can't have good sense."

"After Jones married your niece, did they stay around these parts for long?"

The old woman sat quietly for a moment. "About two years, I reckon. I know she had her first child right over there," the woman said, pointing to a spot underneath the tree. "The house is gone now, but that's where her ma and pa lived, and that's where that boy of hers was born. Sister-gal's boy was a knee baby when that crazy man of hers told everybody that the Lord had called him to preach and he moved her and the child back behind Ridgeland."

Mama stood up. "I appreciate you talking to me, but I reckon we'd better go now," she said.

The woman lowered her voice. "I hear you from the welfare department," the woman said. "Anyway, can you get my pension raised a little?"

Mama smiled sweetly. "I'll check on it," she said.

The woman began laughing, harder and harder. Mama and I inched off the porch and got into the car. When we drove off, the woman was laughing so hard that we were sure she was going to fall out of the rocking chair and through the rotten slats of the old porch.

"Feeble minds run in the family," I whispered.

"I guess I'm going to have to think of another way to get Sister-gal away from her crazy husband," Mama said.

We drove another twenty minutes to Ridgeland, where Mama turned off the highway into the parking lot of the McDonald's that sits beside Interstate 95. It was about three o'clock, and we were both thirsty. We went inside, ordered two large drinks, and found a table. Mama tasted her drink and waited until I had satisfied my own thirst.

"Now, young lady," she said, looking directly into my eyes, "what's the problem you're tackling in Atlanta?"

Chapter 6

Donna's eyes widened; she waved her hands excitedly. "Don't be ridiculous, girlfriend!" she said. "You're kidding me, right?"

"I'm serious as a heart attack," I said. I was thinking of the conversation I'd had with Mama at the McDonald's in Ridgeland. In a concise manner, I had reported the events that had led to my former roommate Cheryl's shooting and killing Harold Young. "I'm serious as a heart attack," I said.

Donna was shaking her head. "Your mother can't come to Atlanta to help you in your work. You're not a little girl who needs her Mama...."

I felt angry. "Wait just one minute," I said. "When I explained to Mama that Cheryl LaFlamme said she had an overwhelming compulsion to kill Harold Young...."

Donna interrupted. "*Girl,* you just don't know. This ain't no place for your mother. You may think she can work some kind of magic in getting down to the bottom of things, but be for real. This is the city, Atlanta, not a country town. You're talking about the murder of a rich and prominent man." Donna was speaking so fast she barely stopped for commas or periods.

I sat quietly for a few seconds. I was trying to control my anger. "Stop right there!" I said. My voice was getting louder. "Mama's magic doesn't work just in Hampton. I told you that my father was in the military and we moved around the world. I've seen Mama work her magic on Japanese, Italians, Spanish, French, rich people as well as poor people. A person's status has nothing to do with Mama's ability. I'm telling you, she's got an uncanny way of solving things."

Donna's chin came up determinedly, but there was no anger in her voice. "But girlfriend, your mother is only a snoop, a self-made private eye with a runaway curiosity. And, in a city like Atlanta, that curiosity could get you and her killed!"

"You're exaggerating. We're not going to take on the Mafia, you know."

Donna's slant eyes blinked.

"I'm paid to look up pertinent information for my boss, information that will help him to defend his clients in a court of law. What's wrong with my allowing Mama to help me do my job, especially if she can find out the information easier and quicker?"

"Okay, okay," Donna said, gesturing as if she was attempting to be more receptive to the idea. "But, even if your mama is so endowed with talent that she can take the sugar out of a cake without breaking a crumb, do you *think* the honorable Mr. Jacoby is going to buy into her so-called 'expertise' and allow you to let her work on his clients?"

I felt my eyebrows lift. "I don't know. I've been trying to figure out how to ask him to let her go with me when I talk to certain people."

Donna threw her head back and laughed. "Girlfriend, take my advice and let your mama stay in Hampton, enjoying her snooping among country folks. She and your father have a nice little house there and she's got a nice little job. She's doing just fine. She's enjoying using her spare time tracking down who stole somebody's chickens or eggs, whichever come first."

"That's not funny!"

Donna's speech slowed down considerably. "Okay, so I'm no comedian. But, your mama ain't no Atlanta detective either. You may be in for a big let-down if you think Mr. Jacoby is going to buy having your mama interview his ultra-rich clients."

"It's not going to cost him anything. I won't be taking her with me often. After all, I'm not trying to get her a job."

"But think, Simone. Mr. Jacoby is a big-time criminal lawyer whose clients have bank accounts beyond our comprehension. Do you really think he's going to risk having you take your mama around talking to people who could cost him the kind of money that would pay your salary for ten years?"

"If I explain…."

Donna laughed cynically. "Explain what? I can hear you now: 'Mr. Jacoby, my mama is a self-proclaimed detective, and I'd like her to accompany me in my work looking out for leads, and/or….'"

"Cool it, Donna," I said in a deadly calm voice.

Donna stared at me for a full ten seconds. "Okay, I'm just trying to be funny, but I seriously think you're doing the wrong thing."

"You never think I'm doing the right thing. I don't know why we're best friends."

Donna rubbed a hand through her thick hair. "I'm your devil's advocate, that's why," she said in a voice that sounded both frustrated and confused.

"You're more like my alter ego."

"The little voice inside you that prods you in the right direction."

I frowned. "The little voice inside me that tries to make me go against what I know is the right thing to do."

Donna lifted her eyebrow. "Excuse me, sister. I was just trying to help."

My frown slowly dissolved into a smile. "It's okay. The fact is that my mama is a powerful woman, and I think you'll have a different impression once you meet her."

We both sat quietly for a while. Donna was wearing a sheer cotton skirt and a bright yellow silk blouse that highlighted her beautiful mocha complexion. She had bright slanted eyes, and I'd often speculated to myself about whether there might be Chinese blood somewhere in her ancestry. Her nose had been altered with surgery, so that couldn't tell me much, but her thick ruby red lips made it clear that she was a soul sister pretty much through and through.

"Got any Diet Cokes?" she asked, her body relaxing noticeably.

I stood up and walked into the kitchen, swearing

under my breath. I don't know why I'm trying to justify myself, I thought. After all, I'm a grown woman. If I want my mother to come visit me, so what? I can't see Mr. Jacoby objecting to her accompanying me to talk to someone who is not even his client. Yeah, I thought as I opened the refrigerator, Mrs. Young is not Mr. Jacoby's client. She is not on trial, and she's not going to give us any information that we're going use in court. I took out two cans of Diet Coke. Donna was totally off base, as usual. I should have never tried to talk it over with her. I walked back into the living room, handed Donna a can, and sat down on the brown chair opposite the leather sofa.

Donna popped open the can of soda. "When is she coming to town?" Her voice was smooth, almost apologetic.

I felt confident. "She's agreed to take off next Wednesday and drive up to Atlanta. I've given her a key to the apartment, and I expect she'll be here when I get home from work. We'll have Thursday and Friday together, and she'll go back home on Saturday."

Donna, toying with the can of soda, leaned forward. "Will you let her meet Cliff?"

"Cliff's working on a divorce case that's got him trotting all over the United States. He's out of town more than he is in, and I don't know if he'll be here or not.

"Girl, are you scared for your mama to meet Cliff?"

"There you go again, Donna. Listen, I'm not putting up with your taking this conversation off into some dark corners of your imagination that have nothing to do with…."

Donna touched my arm. "I'm sorry," she said, her

eyes full of feeling. "Really, I didn't mean anything."

I swallowed. "My mother is a very special lady," I said softly. "I realize that everybody thinks their mama is special, but at least I know what makes mine special. For one thing she's got a way of concealing her thoughts, so most people can't quite figure her out, but that's not all."

Donna took another gulp of soda, swallowed, then let out a long deep breath. "Listen, I don't want to fight about your mother. I'm sure she is a very nice lady, and I'd like very much to meet her when she comes to town. So now...," She leaned back and took another sip from the can. "Tell me about your daddy."

I smiled affectionately. "My father is another kind of beast altogether. I told you he was in the military, so he wasn't home much of the time. But whenever he was at home, he'd always be hugging and kissing us, giving us whatever food or clothing we needed or wanted, and telling us over and over again how he was happy that we were the product of his efforts."

"Sounds like a piece of cake to me."

I grinned. "He is sweet and my mother is crazy about him."

Donna's slanted eyes narrowed, and she tilted her head. "She is?"

I nodded. "Yeah, but not the kind of crazy that she babies him or caters to his every wish. No, she doesn't baby him, but she doesn't neglect him either. They've got kind of a special thing...."

Donna laughed. "Like me and Ernest?" she asked, putting down the empty soda can onto the coffee table next to the sofa.

I leaned back in my chair to give her a long, thorough look. She was an attractive girl. Despite the fact that she got off base at times, I had to admit she was reasonable. At least she was smart enough to know when to push or back off. "Like *we both* would like to have one day when we're Mama's age."

Donna's face softened, just a little. "You got that right," she said.

"How did Ernest's friend enjoy visiting Atlanta?"

"Okay, I guess," Donna admitted. "Ernest said for some reason he didn't think he was as impressed as he thought he would be. Evidently, he got some bad information about Atlanta and things weren't as he expected."

"You know, I never asked: where is he from?"

"New Jersey."

"How did he get a trip to Atlanta?"

"He works for the parent company of the Omni Hotel, just like Ernest does, and he came to town for some training."

"He may be Ernest's friend," I said, shaking my head slowly, "but the man is a dog. All he talked about was all the women he loved that were waiting for him back home."

"Well take heart. Ernest said the same subject was covered extensively in their conversations."

"He'd better get right," I said, remembering the boorish young man. "Times are changing. He may not know it, but he's about to get left behind."

We laughed out loud, stopped laughing by putting our hands over our mouths, then laughed again. Donna began acting out Ernest's friend's physical movements, and I laughed until tears streaked my face. The laughter just kept coming. I would think I had control, then

I'd look at Donna and be off again. I finally went into the bathroom and brought out the box of Kleenex to wipe my eyes.

"Well, at least the evening was worth a good laugh," I said, trying to get control. "I guess it was cheaper than going to a comedy club."

"Ernest said that I don't have to worry about him coming this way again. I don't know what Ernest said to him," Donna explained, wiping her eyes and nose at the same time, "but whatever he whispered into that guy's ear on their way to the airport was enough to guarantee his elimination from our lives for good."

I sniffled and coughed. "Sounds like Ernest took the bull by the horns."

We sat drying our eyes, trying to regain our composure. After a few minutes, Donna spoke. "I told him you weren't going to do him that kind of a favor again, and he admitted that the guy wasn't worth it."

"You know," I smiled, "the more I get to know Ernest, the better I like him. He's an all-right fellow!"

"Well, girlfriend," Donna said, letting out a deep breath. I could see the humor in her eyes as her right eye twitched. She stood up and shot a glance at the clock, then lifted her hand to pat her hair. She bent over and picked up her purse from the sofa, then leaned back slightly on her heels. "The bottom line is that you got to do what you got to do. I don't know what I can do to help you ease your mama onto Mr. Jacoby, but if you think of anything...."

I held my Coke can in front of me in both hands, thinking how wonderful it was that I didn't need Donna's help. Still, at that moment, I realized how important both she and my mother were to me. These two women alone, I thought, are snapshots of me. Donna reflects what I am and my mother reflects what I want to become. The thought, though fleeting, made me feel warm and secure.

Chapter 7

Thursday, August 3

My boss, Mr. Sidney Jacoby, is a white man about sixty, a little heavy but not obese. He has dark brown eyes that can turn warm with compassion or cold with contempt. His teeth gleam; he visits his dentist often, just to have then whitened. He wears his thick naturally curly hair tapered at the neck, and he has his fingernails manicured each and every week. He is a man who dresses impeccably and whose entire domain is in absolute order.

Mr. Jacoby has one flaw: he has constant dandruff that falls from his hair to his shoulders like soft new snow. Everyone who knows him is obliged to flick the dandruff from his hair or his jacket, but for some reason, the little white flakes don't bother him. I often wonder how this man can have such a flair for asking pointed questions and digging out minute details, but can't see the tiny falling flakes that descend from his shoulders like a snow-capped mountain.

Mr. Jacoby and I are, according to his perception, very much alike. He likes to do research, but since he is a very powerful, practicing criminal lawyer who defends high-paying clients by arguing in front of a judge and a jury, he doesn't have the time to spend hours digging up evidence. He says that, even though researching and finding little things that can make or break a case is his real passion, it doesn't pay as well as putting on a show in the courtroom.

Nevertheless, I'm pretty fortunate to work for a man who believes in what I do, supports the way I do it, and pays me very well for doing it. "You're in the trenches, where the action is," he once told me after I had found a note containing several words that proved to be so important that Mr. Jacoby was able to save his client from the electric chair. (The client was indeed innocent; the real murderer was later identified, tried, and convicted.)

"Nobody can tamper with the truth," Mr. Jacoby expounded once. "Simone, if you dig deep enough, peel off all the layers of appearances, cut away through the lies, and strip through the absurdities, you will find the truth, and the high you'll feel from the experience is priceless. Believe me," he added, "I envy you."

And honestly, I believe the man. He feels almost as strongly about finding the truth as Mama does. Now, I'm not saying that I've never seen him stretch the lie, but it has been on very rare occasions. Once, he told me that when he was a boy he was such a stickler for details and finding the truth that he almost drove his mother crazy. He likes to tell the story that when he graduated from college his mother gave him several thousand dollars to get his own apartment.

"You can't come back here," she told him. "I've lived with you for eighteen years, and I *will not* take another day of your questioning everything and everybody. I thank God that you've finally grown up and I don't have to let you live in my house anymore!"

Mr. Jacoby said that his teachers could always count on him to research the little things that they couldn't find time enough to do themselves. And it was to Sidney Jacoby that his peers looked to settle arguments. He never could dance, play sports, or do anything that the other kids called fun, but he knew the details of just about anything and, if he didn't, he wouldn't stop until he found them.

"It's a gift," he once told me, "and don't you ever neglect it or take it for granted. Most people don't have the patience to search for the truth; they'd rather be brainwashed into believing the lie." (By the way, at the same time he gave me a hefty bonus for spending almost three weeks in the courthouse digging up a birth certificate that was so hidden you'd think the person had never been born. Mr. Jacoby believed in paying for the truth.)

One of the favorite times of his life, he says, was when he supported himself through law school by researching information for writers, many of whom made the best seller's list. The little details that he dug up were critical to their work, and they appreciated his industriousness. He never failed to let everybody know that it had been those writers and their friends who made him the very rich criminal trial lawyer that he had become.

Several days before Mama's arrival, I mentioned to Mr. Jacoby that she was coming to town and I wanted him to meet her. He tilted his head and nodded. "I'll note it on my calendar," he said. At the time, I casually reminded him of Mama's savvy when talking to people, but I didn't press too hard. I figured the best way to handle things was to let him meet Mama and get his own impression. Then, I'd suggest that she go with me to the interview I had scheduled with Mrs. Young.

I told Mama about Mr. Jacoby's background, how he loved research, how his forte, when he was in college, had been to research for writers who wrote fiction, non-fiction, and especially mysteries.

The introduction was brief; honestly, I barely remember it. Mama was wearing a beautiful navy blue silk dress that had white trimmings. She had a red silk scarf tucked in at the neck that enhanced her candied sweet potato complexion. She looked stunning. After just a few minutes, she and Mr. Jacoby were deep in the analysis of the methods of Hercule Poirot.

I couldn't believe it. For a while, I sat there speechless, listening to them talk about "little gray cells" and "methods of deduction." Then I tried to break in, to interject something. After all, Mama had spoonfed me on Agatha Christie from birth, but they would have none of it. They kept talking, totally ignoring me, making me feel invisible.

It was then I realized the one thing I *didn't like* about mother. It was the only negative thing that I felt about her sleuthing. It hit me the moment I eased out of Mr. Jacoby's office. There were times when my mother had such a presence that she made me feel like an idiot.

And I wasn't an idiot. As a matter of fact, I whispered as I walked back into my office, I'm the most intelligent person I know.

A little voice in my head whispered, "That is, after Mama."

I laughed out loud. "Oh well," I said to myself as I flopped down into my office chair to patiently await my mother's return, "I guess that's the price I have to pay for her expertise. A bit higher price than I wanted to pay, I admit, but Mr. Jacoby always says that good help deserves good pay, and since I want her help to mesmerize Mrs. Young tomorrow, I have to pay the price of feeling like an idiot in front of my boss." It was one of those little truths that hurt.

It had been almost four o'clock when I had taken Mama into Mr. Jacoby's office. I figured he would give her fifteen minutes; after all, he is a very busy man and it would take only fifteen minutes for Mama's charm to work. Forty-five minutes later my mother was still in the office.

I started getting nervous; I didn't want her to overdo it, as if she could. Lord, I wondered, pacing up and down impatiently in my office, what has that woman talked the man into doing? I heard myself grunt.

Maybe he's making a play for her, I thought.

I smiled, remembering how Mama had handled a tall, good-looking Italian who had been persistent in his attempt to "escort" her out, as he put it. The poor guy didn't know what happened to him. Mama was so gentle, so sweet, and yet so firm that it had been impossible for him to get his feelings hurt. As a matter of fact, if I remembered correctly, he had spent more time apologizing for his impertinence than he had trying to get a date.

Why am I thinking about that now? I wondered, pulling myself back into the present. It was 5:15 P.M.; people were getting ready to leave the office to go home, and neither Mr. Jacoby nor my mother had come out of his office yet.

"She must be pretty important," Carol, Mr. Jacoby's secretary, said. I walked into her office just as she was turning off her typewriter and putting a gray cover over it.

I started pacing up and down in front of her desk. "I don't know what they've got to talk about. They just met for the first time today."

"Well, a few minutes after you walked out of his office, he called me and told me to hold all phone calls, and later he asked me to bring in the file on Cheryl LaFlamme."

"What?"

"She reached inside her desk and pulled out her purse. "When I walked into his office to take Cheryl's file to him, I got the impression...," she said smartly. "But then I could be wrong."

I stopped pacing. "*What* impression did you get?"

She walked past me, toward the door. "I might be wrong."

I spoke fast. "Your impression is worth a free lunch."

"In that case, I heard them talk about collaborating, or something like that."

I sucked my teeth. "Anything more?"

She shook her head.

"Thanks for nothing."

"I want my lunch next week because it's the week between paychecks and I'm kind of strapped."

I nodded perfunctorily.

It was a little past six when Mr. Jacoby and my mother walked out of the office. "I've briefed your mother on the situation," he was saying. "She's promised me a typed report of the interview."

I stared at Mama suspiciously. "What?"

"You are planning to take her with you to visit Mrs. Young tomorrow, aren't you?"

I felt my eyes widen. "If it's okay with you."

"Of course it's okay. As a matter of fact," he said, the dandruff falling down his shoulders elegantly, "I'm most interested in Candi's opinion of Mrs. Young." He looked at Mama and winked.

"What opinion?" I asked, determined to sound self-assured and calm.

"I'll tell you later." Mama smiled engagingly.

"Thanks," I said, taking hold of Mama's arm. "Let's go; we'll be late for dinner."

"Oh, by the way, Candi," Mr. Jacoby said. We both stopped in our tracks. "Remember, you must let me know when you're coming back to town. We'll have dinner."

"Did you hear that man?" I asked as I led my mother to the parking lot where my brightly shined Honda was parked. "He offered to take you to dinner! Mr. Jacoby, the man who has never attended an office party with his own staff, offered to take you to dinner!"

"Well," Mama said, smiling, her eyes twinkling. "We've got a lot in common."

"Mama," I continued, "he doesn't take his own mother out to dinner. They don't like each other. She can't talk to him fifteen minutes without getting pissed."

"Sidney Jacoby's problem with his mother has nothing to do with Cheryl's shooting Harold Young. What Sidney Jacoby and I have in common is the pursuit of the truth. I, at your request, am going to help him find the truth about how Mr. Young died."

"Cheryl shot him, Mama. We know that. What I need you to help me do is find evidence he can use to persuade a jury that there were mitigating circumstances for what she did."

"Are you sure she killed him?"

"She shot him in his office in front of five witnesses!" I shouted.

"Don't you raise your voice at me, young lady," Mama said.

I lowered my voice. "I'm sorry."

"Listen, Simone," Mama said. "I'm going with you in the morning to talk with Harold Young's widow. After that, I'll be in a better position to decide what I can bring to this problem. The one thing I do know now, based on my conversation with Mr. Jacoby and a few things I noticed in the file, is that this case isn't as simple as it appears."

"What do you mean?" I asked.

"I mean there are questions that need to be answered before I'm convinced that Cheryl killed Mr. Young."

"If she didn't kill him, then who did?"

"I don't know. I do know that you and I are going to find out before an innocent young woman is sent to jail." She patted me on the hand. "You and I together," she said. "We're going to get to the truth *before* this case goes to trial."

I was speechless. Whatever had gone down in Mr. Jacoby's office was beyond me. Cheryl had shot and killed Harold Young in his office. There had been five reliable witnesses. Ballistics evidence proved that the bullets that entered Harold Young's body were fired from Cheryl's gun. Cheryl admitted she owned the gun; records showed that she had purchased it from a reputable gun dealer. Cheryl had also admitted that she had called Young at his office that morning. His secretary had told her that Harold Young was unable to speak to her at that time but that he wanted to see her at his office at one o'clock that afternoon. Cheryl admitted that, with the gun in her purse, she had walked into Harold Young's office around 1:05.

Fifteen minutes later, I was trying to maneuver my car in the choking downtown traffic. "One thing that is certain," I said, "is that if Cheryl didn't kill Mr. Young, you and I are going to find out who did." I squeezed through an amber light, hit the brakes, and swerved as a Buick cut me off.

"Take it easy," Mama said, leaning back comfortably in the seat.

Chapter 8

Friday, August 4

Though it was barely ten o'clock in the morning, the sky was already brilliant. The warmth and light filtered through the trees as we turned into the driveway of the home of Mrs. Harold Young. Cedars guarded each side of the drive, arching overhead, transforming the lane into a cool, dim tunnel. The sun filtered through sporadically, throwing patches of light on the ground. The house stood at the end of the drive, two stories of brick surrounded by azaleas, dogwoods, and gardenias. Ivy clung to columns, and iron grillwork encircled a balcony like delicate black lace.

When we were halfway up the driveway, I noticed a man who had been working in the yard walking toward us. He wore faded jeans and a blue shirt. His sleeves were rolled to his elbow, and his collar was open. His mud-stained fingers were long. I stopped the car but left it in gear with the engine running. I rolled the window down.

"Who are you looking for?" he asked, his stare long and cold.

Mama smiled. "Mrs. Young," she said.

A muscle twitched in the corners of the man's mouth. "Is she expecting you?"

Mama's warm smile was getting to him. I could see his face relaxing a little. "Yes, she is. As a matter of fact, we're a few minutes late now."

He stepped back. "Go on then."

I glanced in the rearview mirror as I drove the remainder of the long drive. He stood watching us, his shoulders slouched, his arms folded. When we rang the doorbell, a housekeeper answered the door. She was a black woman, whose skin looked weathered and worn. She had deep lines in her face, and she wore her hair in a knot at the back of her neck.

She ushered us into a large study that was decorated with bric-a-brac and items that seemed unnatural and out of place. The fireplace and a large window were the room's focal points. The entire room, especially it's vast size, reminded me of something out of a gothic castle.

From the moment Mrs. Young walked into the room, it was obvious that she was far from devastated by her husband's death. An efficient, businesslike woman, she had eyes that seemed cold and without any sense of pain or loss. She had a pasty white complexion, a nose that turned up, and though she was small, she was a little heavy in the bust. She spoke in an unhurried and deliberate manner, as if she had rehearsed for our visit. Mama had said, before we rang the doorbell, that the fact that she was letting us visit her this morning in her home was testimony that she had suffered no deep loss at her husband's death. My first look at the woman convinced me that Mama was right again.

"Mrs. Young…," I tried smiling amiably. "We appreciate your giving us this opportunity to meet with you this morning."

Mrs. Young eyed us both suspiciously. When she spoke, her tone was sharp but she was not snobbish. "My sister-in-law and her lawyer explicitly advised that I *not* speak to you. What exactly do you want?" she asked.

Mama opened her bag, pulled out a lace-trimmed handkerchief, sniffed, and blew her nose. "We don't want anything, Mrs. Young," she said, her voice relaxed and natural, "and *I am* terribly sorry about your husband's tragic death."

Mrs. Young's eyebrows rose noticeably. "It *was* tragic," she said. Something in her voice made me wonder if that fact hadn't occurred to her before Mama had said it. "I can't understand why that young woman had to do such a thing."

"It must have been a shock to find out that the same young woman you'd met on your trip to the Bahamas was the very one who killed your husband," Mama continued.

She looked at both Mama and me as she spoke. "It's the only reason I agreed to talk to you. I still can't believe it. She was such a pleasant young woman. Harold was kind enough to her. I can't understand it!"

Mrs. Young's voice softened, her eyes were distant, remembering. "She and her friend Penny were both very nice young ladies, especially on the island of

73

Nassau. We spent a great deal of time together, the three of us, since Harold spent most of the time locked up in the hotel room, talking on the telephone to his office here in Atlanta. You know that I asked the girls to permit me to spent some time with them exploring the island."

She smiled reminiscently. "We had a pretty good time. One night the three of us went down into the lounge, and those silly girls...." She stopped without finishing the sentence. "I must admit," she continued, "that they both contributed a great deal to *my* vacation."

"You never got the impression that Cheryl wanted to hurt your husband?" I asked.

"Of course not," Mrs. Young snapped, regaining her stoic attitude. "It's hard to believe even now that she...."

Mama spoke. "I've never visited the Bahamas, but I hear it's a tropical paradise, a perfect place for a vacation."

Mrs. Young stood up, walked over toward a table where several glasses and a tumbler were neatly arranged. We watched her pour herself a drink. She sipped from the glass, and I noticed that her shoulders relaxed a little. She did not return to her seat but walked to the window and stood with her back to us, looking out across the lawn. "It is a beautiful island," she said. "I'd made plans for the trip several times before, but Harold was always too busy to get away."

"That's the way it is when you've got a husband," Mama said. "My husband was a career military man and it was always difficult to plan things. Whenever I planned things for us, Uncle Sam would find something else for James to do. I remember once…."

Mrs. Young turned, walked slowly back to the sofa, and sat down. "It was always hard for me to believe that Harold couldn't have gotten away for a vacation," she said, interrupting Mama's remarks.

I had realized from the expression on Mama's face that she wanted to elicit more of Mrs. Young's opinions about her husband. Mama smiled, using a technique of smiling without opening her mouth and at the same time looking directly into Mrs. Young's eyes. Mama always allowed a silence when she did this, and after a few moments I could see that Mrs. Young's shoulders begin to relax. "Would you like a glass of water?" Mrs. Young offered.

Mama shook her head but said nothing.

"You'd think Harold had to work day and night…." She paused, her voice slightly bitter. "You'd think that making money was the only thing that mattered to him."

"Maybe," Mama said (in her I-understand-what-you-mean voice), "that your husband came from a family with strong work ethics?"

Mrs. Young looked up from her drink. Out of the corner of my eyes, I could see her fingers gripping the glass. She took another sip, put the glass back on the small table, and averted her eyes from Mama's face. "The only person I know in my husband's family is my sister-in-law, and I really don't know that much about her. She and Harold never discussed their family history," she said, almost too calmly.

"Usually," Mama said, in the manner of two women chitchatting, "when a man works all the time, it's because his family viewed work as some kind of moral code that carries a stiff penalty if it's broken."

Mrs. Young smiled. "Maybe," she said. "We were together for twenty-five years. When we first got married, he politely evaded my questions, but after a while, he ignored them."

"Did you know your husband long before your marriage?" Mama asked.

A pink blush flushed on Mrs. Young's cheeks. "I met Harold in college, a few months before graduation, to be exact. He was a wonderful man: warm, sensitive, generous. More than that, he had vision and a quick mind. I felt fortunate that he would date me. There were so many other girls after him, you know. As it turned out, he literally swept me off of my feet, and six months after we had graduated, he asked me to marry him."

"I suppose his family couldn't get to the wedding?" Mama asked.

Mrs. Young shook her head. "His sister attended our marriage ceremony," she said. "Harold and I decided against a church wedding." She paused. "We had a civil ceremony."

"Twenty-five years is a long time," Mama said, changing the direction of the conversation. "Despite the tragedy of your husband's death, nobody can take the memory of those years away from you."

When Mrs. Young spoke, her voice was calm, but I could see that her cheeks were quivering. "To a great extent, they were good years," she said. "Basically, we lived an uncomplicated life. Harold had no hobbies, no friends. He always insisted that he was an ordinary man who wanted to live an ordinary life. He was kind and gentle, and sometimes I thought him quite dull. Who would have believed he had an enemy?"

"I am sorry," Mama said, her voice sounding genuinely concerned. "I wish I could say something that would make the loss of your husband less painful."

Mrs. Young sat silently for a few moments, her face almost serene. She looked down at her hands. "It's funny," she said when she finally spoke, her voice in a whisper. "There is no real pain, not even sadness. Isn't that odd? Harold was a kind, gentle man, sweet and caring in every way, but for some reason, I'm not even lonely without him. Now that he's dead, the only thing in my life that has changed is that he's gone. Don't you think it's strange that, after twenty-five years of marriage, there is no pain, no feeling of loss?"

Mama looked at her watch and nodded.

It's difficult enough to try to comfort somebody in mourning over a loved one, but what do you say to a woman who can't understand why she isn't mourning the tragic death of a husband of twenty-five years? I began feeling uncomfortable.

I cleared my throat. "We'd better go," I said, rising from my chair and looking around the room. "We appreciate your valuable time, Mrs. Young."

Mama continued to sit firmly in place, blind to my gesture to leave. She leaned forward toward Mrs. Young, almost as if she didn't want me to hear what she was saying. "If you'd like," Mama said, her voice compelling, "I'll come back and we'll talk more."

Mrs. Young didn't reply but looked at Mama appreciatively and nodded. There were tears in her eyes, and I stared, puzzled since she had just said that she didn't feel the loss of her dead husband. Mama stood up, punched me in the side, and directed me back through the hall and out the front door. Outside the sun was

77

blinding, and we hurriedly put on our sunglasses.

When we pulled out of the driveway, I looked back toward the house. The old man was still working in the yard, his lined face and graying hair testifying to a hard life.

"I wonder," I said to Mama, "what kind of woman could be married to a man for twenty-five years and not feel the pain of his death?"

"I don't know," Mama said, introspectively. "But mark my words, there's something profound behind those dark eyes of Mrs. Young's."

We drove in silence for several minutes as I maneuvered a curve up a hill. When the car started down the hill, Mama spoke again. "I want you to ask Mr. Jacoby to arrange for you and me to talk to Cheryl next Saturday."

"Why?"

"I want to know more about how Mr. and Mrs. Young interacted on their Bahamas vacation," she replied.

Chapter 9

Friday, August 18

It took a couple of weeks for Mr. Jacoby to work our schedules to arrange for me and Mama to visit Cheryl.

While driving to her apartment, I remembered that Cheryl had left school after the first semester. We had vowed to keep in touch. Neither of us had kept the promise. It had been over five years. And, although I couldn't say we were best friends, I still thought of her as more than an acquaintance.

I must admit I felt a warmth mixed with apprehension when I knocked on Cheryl's door. Mr Jacoby was right: I was beginning to feel more connected to my work. Cheryl was not just a client who needed an alibi; she was a friend in trouble.

Cheryl lived in Atlanta's DeKalb county, near Stone Mountain. When Cheryl opened the door, she gave me a bear-hug, clearly genuinely delighted to see me again. She was clinging to me so tightly that we had to stumble inside her living room of cool, clean air. She was wearing a white cotton skirt and a royal blue cotton T-shirt.

She gave me a long warm look, a loving smile.

I responded. "Girl, you look good."

"You look great too," she said. She reached out her hand toward Mama. "So this is your mother."

"Yeah," I said. "You know, the one I spoke so fondly of when we were in college."

Mama looked at me and rolled her eyes. She looked at Cheryl and smiled. Cheryl said something while waving us into chairs.

I had remembered Cheryl as being a very pretty woman, but today she was radiant. Her long auburn hair, big green eyes, and flawless ivory skin shined. Her manner, her voice and her way of sitting made it clear that she had not been born into wealth even though she smelled of expensive bath oil and perfume. It was hard to imagine this woman killing an animal, much less shooting a man in cold blood.

I blinked. "You know, I've never met *your* family," I said.

She cleared her throat, the enthusiasm faded out of her face. "My parents are dead," she said. "They were both ill for so long. When they died, I had to borrow money to bury them." Cheryl brushed her hair back from her face. "You know, I was adopted."

I nodded.

There were tears in her eyes. "They were both nice people."

"Do you remember much about your childhood?"

"I remember being adopted, living in a small house that my new mother kept clean and neat." She stared toward the cat.

"I'm sorry," Mama said.

Cheryl closed her eyes.

"I don't remember your having many friends," I said absently.

Cheryl opened her eyes. "It took all I could do to make it through school and pay off funeral debts," she confessed. "I didn't have time to make friends." She smiled, "Since I've been working though, I've got one friend. Her name is Penny. She went on the vacation trip with me."

I smiled. "Well, now that we're here, you've got two more."

"Thanks," she said warmly. "I need you both." Her voice became somber. "I can't explain how this thing happened. It's like a nightmare. For a lifetime I felt nothing; I was like a zombie, the living dead. Then one look into an old man's eyes and I'm flooded with repulsive excitement. Nobody can imagine what I went through the months before the shooting…."

"It must have been horrible," I said.

Her face had turned a sort of chalk white. "You know," she said, "I never told Dr. Joyce about Harold Young."

"Why?"

Cheryl drew a deep, shuddering breath and then straightened up in her chair. "I was scared," she said.

"She might have helped you handle it differently."

She shook her head. "Every time I tried, I got a lump, like a fist, in my throat." Cheryl gave me a feeble smile. "I might have wanted to kill him," she said.

81

"You *wanted* to kill Harold Young?" I asked.

She shook her head. "I don't know," she said; a nerve twitched high up on her cheek. "I watched both my parents die. They suffered so much the idea of death is not abhorrent. To me, it means peace, serenity, freedom...."

There was a silence. Then Mama leaned forward. "Before you met Harold Young, did you remember anything about your life prior to your adoption?"

Cheryl looked toward the ceiling. "I remembered somebody bathing me, screaming that I must always stay clean."

"Anything else?"

Cheryl straightened and nodded.

"Was there any indication that you had been sexually molested prior to your seeing Mr. Young?" Mama asked.

Cheryl looked at Mama with a pitying expression. "Before I saw Harold Young on the plane, I felt nothing sexually..., absolutely nothing. That's what frightened me. Then I felt a sensuousness that I had never even imagined; it made me sick."

Nobody spoke for the next few moments. I looked around the living room. Cheryl's apartment had been decorated in earth tones: browns and greens, with dashes of yellow and red.

A black and white cat jumped to the deep window sill, where he sat, back turned to us, looking out at the huge mountain that looms over the entire area.

"Why did you leave school after the first semester?" I asked.

She sighed, raising a hand to hike her hair. "Money," she said amiably. "It had always eluded me. After my first semester in college," she turned to me directly, "I had to go to work full time. I finished at night."

I nodded.

I broke a croissant, loaded it with marmalade, and nibbled at it.

Cheryl spoke slowly in a low voice, almost as if she was talking to herself. I felt I couldn't ask her to speak louder, so I had to lean forward to hear her. "The journey from being a waitress to becoming an executive has been a hard one."

She started pouring coffee into our cups. She had set the cream, sugar, butter, marmalade, and croissants on the glass-topped table earlier. "It seemed to take me forever to finish college," she said. Suddenly, Cheryl looked more uncomfortable. "It was worth it," she said. "My parents would have been proud."

Mama leaned back in her chair as if she was contemplating something. "What made you decide on the vacation?" she asked.

Cheryl looked down at her slender hands. "My shrink," she said. "The eminent Dr. Joyce had been after me to get on with the personal side of my life, to find my prince charming, you know." She paused for a moment and then added, "She's been trying to help me break though a fear of intimacy."

Mama nodded thoughtfully.

Cheryl raised her head. "After all," she continued, looking at us with wide eyes, "I'm an attractive woman, don't you think?"

Mama nodded again. She took another sip of the very good hot coffee and stared, waiting for Cheryl to continue speaking.

Cheryl glanced toward the cat. "I'm a virgin," she

admitted, her voice subdued and thoughtful. "In this age of promiscuity that's like having some kind of disease."

I leaned forward in the chair; I felt strangely sisterly toward this white woman. "It's a personal thing," I said. "You don't have to be ashamed of your virginity."

The cat turned away from the window, stretched out a rear leg, and, neck arched, began to wash its stomach.

Cheryl leaned back in her chair. "Dr. Joyce said it's because of my repressed background," she said, "but I didn't believe her."

"And now?" Mama asked.

There was pain in her eyes. "I don't know," she said. "I just know how Harold Young made me feel, and that feeling was so strong that I couldn't...."

Cheryl got up and carried her empty cup over to the sink.

Mama's eyebrow rose; she crossed her legs unhurriedly.

Cheryl stood staring toward the window. "You'd think a woman who has worked her way up to a plush office like mine...." She stopped. "Well, anyway," she sighed, "Dr. Joyce thought that a vacation would be the thing to help me with the process." Cheryl whispered thoughtfully, "It was the first time I'd ever taken a vacation."

Mama's voice was quiet, calm, almost hypnotic. "What made you decide on the Bahamas?" she asked.

Cheryl relaxed a degree and sat back down. "My friend Penny picked the package. She has always had fantasies of meeting a tall, dark, handsome man in the

Caribbean islands."

"When did you begin to realize that Harold Young was familiar?" Mama asked, her voice soft and steady.

"The whole thing is burned in my memory," she said, her voice shaking and tears welling up in her eyes.

"When I walked down the aisle of the plane, trying to locate my seat, I looked down into a thin, angular face with high cheekbones and full lips; light eyes…, blue or hazel. I smiled, and suddenly my body felt a stir of sexual stimulation. I felt sick, a tightness in my chest, the same feeling I have whenever I hear thunder. I can remember when I was young I would rush outside to stare anxiously at the clouds. If their undersides were dark gray and thick and rolling, I would run back inside to hide my head under my pillow. That day, the terror I felt was as real as a thunderstorm, but I couldn't run and hide. I couldn't even move down the aisle. Penny thought I had become airsick, so she took me by the arm and led me to our seats. She reached into her purse and offered me a Dramamine tablet. Even though my stomach was doing leaps, I declined.

"Next, we put our overnight cases in the hatches above, sat down in the plane, and began fastening our seatbelts. I tried to look at the man's face again, but it was impossible to see him from where I sat. I could see a woman, about his age, sitting next to him. He's got a traveling companion, I thought. I closed my eyes, fighting the pull of desire. I had to know his name.

"A few minutes later, Penny nudged me, and asked, 'What is the matter with you?'

"'Nothing,' I said. 'It's just that man makes me feel funny. I know I've seen him before.'

"She said, 'From the look you've just given him,

you'd think he reminded you of someone that you never wanted to see again.'

"After the plane was in the air, I fled to the ladies' room, standing inside the door with my hands to my face. Something about the man made me feel vulnerable; the worst of it was the sexual desire. I returned to the seat. The stewardess came down the aisle and leaned over and asked me, 'Are you all right?'

"'I'm fine, thank you,' I said, fastening my seatbelt.

"'See,' Penny said as the stewardess continued up the aisle. 'You do look sick.'

"'I'm okay,' I said. The plane reached cruising altitude and the stewardess began serving meals and drinks. I had little to say during the trip because I couldn't quiet my mind, my feelings. When we stopped over in Miami, I did everything possible to keep the man and woman in sight. When Penny saw that I was staring again, she jumped all over me.

"'Stop staring,' she said. 'What's with you anyway? Why can't you stop staring at that man?'

"'I don't know,' I said. 'I can't help myself. I don't mean to do it.'

"'You're embarrassing me. I don't want that woman to come and hit you over the head for staring at her husband.'

"'I'm sorry,' I said. 'I'll try to control myself.'

"'Take it easy kid,' Penny joked. 'The travel agent guaranteed that there will be at least two single, handsome guys in the Bahamas just for us.'

"It turned out that our travel plans were identical with the Youngs'. When we were boarding the ship, I followed my impulse and bumped into the man.

"'Excuse me,' I said, looking into his eyes.

"He stared coolly. 'Do I know you?' he asked.

"This was the first flicker of memory…. I remembered hearing my voice, crying, pleading. 'No,' I stammered. 'I don't think so.'

"His eyes looked wild; I felt myself tremble. 'I don't think so either,' he said, again pausing after each word. 'I told my wife that I'd never met you. She wondered why you're staring at me.'

"I felt a lightness at the pit of my stomach; I turned away. 'I'm sorry,' I whispered."

Cheryl lifted her hair from her neck; she was biting her lower lip. "There was something frightening in his eyes that made me feel a sickening jolt."

It was several minutes before Mama spoke. The three of us sat at the table, thinking about what Cheryl had just recounted. Cheryl chewed her lip, a habit that had annoyed me when we had been roommates.

Mama leaned forward in her chair. "He must have been talking pretty loud," she said quietly. "According to the legal depositions, Penny, Mrs. Young, and the ship's purser heard that conversation."

Cheryl made a face. "He wasn't talking that loud, but he was breathing hard. I guess people nearby noticed how, after he spoke a word, he'd take one deep breath then push air from his lips."

I had to admit, Cheryl's account was exactly as she had given it in her official deposition, which was in our office files. I wanted to believe her, but I remembered how, when she was in college, she could memorize verbatim entire chapters of books.

"How did you get to know his wife?" Mama asked.

"Mr. Young didn't come out of his cabin much," Cheryl said, "so his wife Irene spent most of the time alone on the ship. Penny and I were alone most of the time. The travel agent had lied: there were very few single men on the cruise. When we were about to leave the ship, Irene approached Penny and me. 'I'm sorry for my husband's rudeness,' she said. 'He's not feeling well and....'

"'My friend isn't feeling well either,' Penny told her, nudging me.

"'He likes to think of himself as inconspicuous.'

"'He reminds me of somebody,' I told her, 'but I can't remember who.'

"'Don't worry about it,' she said, smiling gracefully. 'I'm sure you'll remember that the person you're thinking about is somebody else. If you haven't met Harold through his firm, J. Higgins & Sons, you haven't met him. He hasn't been well for the past ten years, so we don't get out much. It's his office or his home.'

"'I know the type,' Penny whispered, looking at me mockingly.

"'You're not a workaholic, are you?' Irene Young asked.

"'Not anymore,' I told her. 'I'm on vacation and I'm going to have a good time.'

"'Good,' she said, patting my arm and walking away.

"After we left the ship, I lost sight of both Harold and Irene. The next day, I spotted Irene in the hotel's gift shop. This time, I approached her. 'We seem to be drawn together,' I joked.

"'It's probably a good thing for me,' she said. 'My husband is upstairs in bed.'

"I smiled.

"'I don't want to impose,' Irene said, 'but I wonder

if it'll be all right for me to tag along with you and your friend? I've wanted this trip for a long time, and I'd like to see as much of the island as possible.'

"I was elated. I ran up to the room and told Penny. She wasn't too thrilled, but she didn't object. After all, she thought, if we found two guys we'd simply explain to Mrs. Young that she was a third wheel. So, the remainder of the vacation, we spent touring the island from end to end. Whenever I asked about Mr. Young, Irene simply said that he wasn't feeling well.

"Three days into the vacation another ship visited the island, and Penny and I did meet two young men. Irene took the hint and gave us space, but when possible she trotted along with us. The only thing she told me about her husband was that he was an executive vice president for J. Higgins & Sons, a clothier, and that he worked day and night. I learned that they had been married for twenty-five years, had no children, and hadn't taken a vacation for almost twenty years.

"I also learned that Irene had graduated college, had married Harold six months later, and a year later had inherited a fortune due to the death of her parents and older brother in a private plane crash. Her passion was writing; she was the author of several novels that had been published, though none had become best sellers. She wanted to write a non-fiction travel book; thus her interest in going to the Bahamas."

"Did you see Mr. Young at any other time?" Mama asked.

Cheryl sighed heavily and nodded. "Occasionally, he'd come down out of his room and eat in the hotel restaurant. Every time I looked into his face, I felt a strange, restless energy pulling at my body."

"Did you talk to him again?"

"No," Cheryl said, without breaking eye contact.

"What happened on the ship back from the vacation?"

"Nothing. It turned out that two days before the ship was to return to the island to pick us up, Harold and Irene boarded an airplane and flew back to the states."

"Why?"

"I guess Harold Young was sick," Cheryl said. "Irene called us at our room and said that her husband needed to get back to see his doctor."

"How did you get their address?"

"I asked Irene for her address and telephone number," Cheryl replied.

"Did you ever get the impression that Mr. Young might have remembered you?" Mama asked.

Cheryl hesitated. "Once," she finally answered. "The day before he flew home. I remember thinking that he looked like he remembered me, but it passed quickly."

Mama smiled sweetly.

Cheryl pressed her lips together hard; she looked troubled. "I know," she said, in disgust, "that what I had been feeling for Harold Young made me feel so dirty that I could never be clean, and I hated him for it!"

Mama stood up, preparing to leave, and I followed.

Chapter 10

Friday, August 25

I looked across the table. I was sitting in my parents' kitchen, enjoying my mother's Saturday morning feast of a breakfast. There were scrambled eggs, biscuits, country sausages, marmalade, and fresh peaches (sliced and sprinkled with cinnamon and sugar).

"Well, Simone," Daddy said, "one more week before our vacation starts. Your mama and I are going to spend two whole weeks home together."

"Do you have plans?" I asked.

"Not really," Mama said, shaking her head.

"I've got some things I want to do around the house," Daddy said. "Things I've been putting off for a long time."

Mama nodded.

"Will it take you the entire two weeks?" I asked.

"Why?" Mama asked

"Because I want you to meet a friend," I said, picking up a biscuit and spreading marmalade thickly on top. "His name is Cliff."

There was a short silence. Both my parents stared at me.

"Is he the young man whose pictures are scattered generously about your apartment?" Mama asked, her voice sounding naturally charming.

Daddy started to raise a fork to his mouth, then hesitated. "Is he the same one who keeps your Honda running like a top?" he asked.

"To answer both questions," I said, leaning back in my chair, "he's one and the same."

My parents glanced at each other, but neither spoke a word. Mama sipped her coffee. Daddy swallowed the mouthful of country sausage he had chewed, then cleared his throat. "Is it serious?" he asked.

"It's serious enough for both of you to get to know him."

Daddy's face was thoughtful. He toyed with his fork for a moment. "When did you have in mind?" he asked.

"Maybe you both can come and spend a week with me. Next week is the Labor Day weekend," I said. "If you come to Atlanta on Saturday, you can stay until the following Saturday, and we can plan something."

Daddy's eyes widened. "Why can't you bring him here?" he asked.

Mama finished her coffee and set the cup down slowly and deliberately. "We'd love to spend a week in Atlanta," she said.

Daddy, disappointed, looked inquiringly around the table. "Why Atlanta? I've got things to do right here."

"I can use a week in Atlanta," Mama answered.

Daddy slumped back in his chair. "You've been going to Atlanta regularly now for the past six weeks," he said. "With all the driving you do within the county for the welfare department, and now with your frequent trips to Atlanta, you're putting a lot of mileage on that car. I wasn't planning on buying another car for several more years."

Mama sighed. "Let's plan to go to Atlanta for the first week," she said, choosing her words carefully. "We'll still have another entire week to spend at home together. Besides, it'll be nice for you to get away for a change. We haven't gotten away together for almost a year. You'll enjoy seeing the things that Simone has done to her apartment."

Daddy got very quiet and still. "We'll see," he said, brooding.

Mama's brow wrinkled. "They found Sister-gal dead yesterday," she said, changing the subject."

I leaned toward Mama. "What?" I asked.

Daddy scratched his head. "What did she die of?" he asked.

"She was beaten and left for dead, then the old shack was set on fire. Sister-gal, with her last bit of strength, crawled free from the burning house, but she died anyway. When they found her, she had been dead for hours."

"Where's her old man?" I asked.

"Nobody knows. He and the children have disappeared," she said

Daddy frowned. "They're probably holed up in some woods back behind Ridgeland," he said.

"Well," I asked, almost accusingly, "what are you going to do now?"

Mama didn't seem to take offense. "I've got several people keeping an eye out for him," she said. "I want you and James," she looked at Daddy pleadingly, "to drive out to the Jones place with me this afternoon."

"For pete sake why?" Daddy asked.

"I don't know," Mama said. "I just know I need to go out there. I've got a feeling that I should go today."

"The fire is probably still smoldering," Daddy commented. "The ashes will be too hot for you to get near the place. And that's none of your business. The sheriff can take care of finding Sister-gal's murderer!"

Mama took a deep breath. "James," she said, "I know that this business is not your cup of tea, but I want you to go out there with me anyway."

Daddy sighed. "I've got plans," he said angrily, "and I can't change them. "Maybe sometime tomorrow afternoon I'll drive out there with you."

Mama looked at me. "I don't think it's a good idea for you and me to go out there alone," I said quickly. "Suppose both of those men are near. We couldn't do much if they attacked us together."

Daddy stood up and walked over to the window. "What time did you plan to go out there?" he asked.

"Whatever time that's convenient for you," Mama answered, putting the dishes into the sink. She started running dishwater, picked up the bottle of Ivory liquid, squeezed several times, and put the bottle back underneath the kitchen sink.

Daddy breathed heavily for a few seconds. "I've got to be back home before two o'clock, Candi," he finally said. "I've got an important appointment, and I don't plan to miss it because you want to go snooping around in somebody's old burned-out shack."

Mama looked at the clock. "It's just ten o'clock now," she said. "I can see no reason for us not to be back to Hampton by two o'clock."

"I'll be ready to leave in about an hour," Daddy said. "I've got to check something on my truck."

Mama looked at me, smiled, then turned toward the kitchen sink to wash her dishes. I started to follow Daddy out of the house but instead decided to help her with the dishes. After all, I thought, she'll be coming to Atlanta for three days next weekend, and I would want her to cook several meals for us.

It was twelve o'clock when we drove up to the ruins of the Jones shack. Daddy was right: in this August heat, the ashes were still smoldering. Mama instructed Daddy to drive down a deep-rutted, narrow road that was almost hidden by weeds. The road ended abruptly in a spot that appeared far from any sign of human habitation. Mama got out of the car and began walking toward a thin path that led into the back of the woods.

"Where are you going?" Daddy asked.

"Follow me," Mama said. "There's another path that leads out into the woods. I bet that old man or the boy is hiding back behind those trees." She pointed to an overgrown tangle of woods. The three of us inched down the thin path, surrounded by trees, bramble bushes, weeds, and poison ivy. Flies, mosquitoes, and gnats swarmed around our necks and faces. Despite the heat of the August day, I felt my flesh shiver and my left leg cramp, along with cuts, bruises, aches, and stings. My face and neck began to feel like it was on fire, with sharp little cuts from low hanging tree limbs. I felt like screaming from pain. Oddly, my father didn't say

95

much. He acted like he was in charge and that it was his mission to keep control over the situation. Mama kept pushing ahead, as if she knew exactly where she was headed.

By the time we stopped, we were standing in a small clearing where several cardboard boxes were slashed down and laid flat out on the ground. On top of the cardboard were rags and what looked like an old blanket. Next to the blanket were several jugs of water, a kerosene lamp, and a stack of wood and several beer cans.

Daddy signaled us to get down on our hands and knees, and we obeyed. "Stay put," he ordered. We complied as he inched his way toward the makeshift abode. He looked around cautiously, then returned to the edge of the clearing to join Mama and me.

"It's the boy," he said.

"How do you know?" I whispered.

"The indentation on the bed, the footprint...." He stopped. "Why am I explaining this to you?" he snapped.

"I know it's the boy," Mama interrupted. "But where is he now?"

"I don't know, but we'll go back the way we came, notify the sheriff, and...."

"He'll be gone by then," Mama warned impatiently.

"No he won't," Daddy said. "Now listen, Candi." His voice was firm. "This is out of our league. We're going to get the law."

Out of the corner of my eye, at that very moment, I saw a shadowy figure. I motioned to Daddy, who waved for us to step back into the woods.

I held my breath.

"He hasn't seen us," Daddy said. "I'm going to try to grab him from behind. For God sake, be quiet."

For the next few minutes, Mama and I sat in the woods watching Daddy, inch by inch, move toward the unsuspecting form. I took a deep breath and prayed that we wouldn't get snakebitten. As Daddy crawled on the other side of the woods, we watched the boy plunder through a croaker sack, pulling out bread and meat. He was eating ravenously and appeared so engrossed in his meal that he didn't pay attention to any of the sounds or movements around him.

"He probably stole some food," Mama whispered.

I swallowed and nodded, remembering Daddy's instructions to keep quiet.

The boy spun around just as Daddy tried to grab him from behind. He lunged forward, trying to push past Daddy. Daddy's military training went into action. He reached out and caught the boy by the shoulder and punched him hard in his stomach. The boy fell down on his knees, then jumped up to run, but Daddy grabbed him again, this time around the waist, and they both fell down, rolling around on the red clay ground.

The boy struggled in blind panic, his arms and legs flinging wildly. He tried to fight his way out of Daddy's grip, but it was obvious that his strength was ebbing. After a few more minutes, Daddy's strong arms were around the boy's waist, and a few moments later Daddy had straddled him. The boy screamed in hysterics.

"Get me something to tie his hands," Daddy ordered, breathing hard. I could see that his face was bruised. "Calm down," he shouted at the boy.

Mama looked around, ran over and grabbed the croaker sack, and threw its contents onto the ground.

She tore it into several pieces, giving them to Daddy, who used them efficiently to control the boy.

After the boy stopped screaming, everything was quiet. I looked down at him. You would have thought he had gone into a trance. His vacant eyes stared toward the edge of the woods. He was short, with a long, pinched-in nose and a small, bitter mouth. He had a high forehead and bulging popped eyes.

Mama's eyes twinkled. "We'd better get back," she said, looking at her watch. "It's 1:15. It'll take every bit of forty five minutes to get back to Hampton and deliver our goods to Sheriff Abe."

Daddy stood staring toward a ditch at the end of the dark and ominous woods.

"What's the matter?" Mama asked.

"Something's dead in that ditch," he said.

A tremor of anxiety swept through me.

"How do you know?" Mama asked.

He cocked his head slightly. "The smell," he said. "I'll always remember the smell of dead flesh."

We walked toward the ditch bank and stood immobilized, our hearts beating in our throats. The water was brownish green; the flesh was black and naked. We took a few steps closer and saw that her hands were tied behind her back. The child's face was swollen beyond recognition, the eyes were sockets; the cheeks, lips, and jaw gnawed and torn by predators of the night.

I backed away a few steps. Daddy moaned painfully. Mama started rubbing her hands together. The boy blinked and stared up at us with loathing in his eyes, and I remember feeling like I was in the presence of pure evil. Suddenly he hollered, "Papa!"

We looked around. A moment later, we saw a man

standing, his shoulders hunched, at the edge of the woods. He looked like a bear. His black beard and wooly hair were long and dirty. He disappeared before Daddy could make a move toward him.

Chapter 11

Saturday, September 2
(Labor Day Weekend)

"Have they come any closer to finding Reverend Jones?" I asked Mama.

It was just after lunch and we were in Atlanta, in my apartment. Mama was sitting on the leather sofa and I sat in the black leather chair. Several brown folders, stacked with legal documents about Cheryl, covered the glass-and-chrome coffee table that stood between us.

Daddy had gone out to explore the neighborhood. It would be another five hours before Cliff, Donna, and Ernest would be coming for dinner.

"No," Mama answered.

"He's probably hiding out in the woods," I said.

"It's a funny thing about that situation," Mama said. "Few people would talk to me about Reverend Jones."

"That's strange," I said. "You're supposed to be able to crack the hardest nut."

Mama rolled her eyes. "The few people who did talk to me said that they don't believe Jones is a killer."

"You've got to be kidding."

"They seem to think somebody else is responsible for the things that have happened."

"Who?"

"I don't know," Mama said. "But I'm beginning to suspect that there is more to this thing with the Jones family than meets the eye."

"What are you going to do?"

"I don't know yet. Right now," she said, changing the subject, "explain to me once again exactly what happened when Cheryl shot Harold Young."

"According to her story," I said, "Cheryl began stalking Harold Young right after she returned from vacation. She said that she followed him whenever she could, getting up early in the morning just to see what time he left home for work. According to her, the only two places he spent any time were his home and his office…. He'd leave for the office early every morning and return to his house every night between eight and nine o'clock.

"A couple of times, she said, he stopped at a book store, you know the kind that sells both books and magazines. Once, she followed him to a doctor's office, but he only stayed a few minutes. Other than that, he kept a direct path back and forth from work.

"Slowly, as she stalked the man, her memory began to return. It was clear in her mind that she'd known him as a child, that he had touched her private parts, that she had loathed him. She had to confront him, so she decided to call him and tell him what she was beginning to remember.

"The morning of the murder, around eleven o'clock, she called his office, but he refused to talk to her directly. Instead, his secretary told her that he was unable to talk to her on the phone but that he wanted her to come to his office that afternoon around one o'clock.

"Cheryl said she had bought the automatic pistol several weeks earlier, but she swears that she didn't plan to kill Young. She said the gun helped her cope with the helplessness she was beginning to experience. Anyway, she said she didn't remember putting the gun in her purse before she left to go to Young's office.

"When she got to his office, she said that his secretary (who confirmed this part of the story) pressed the intercom button and announced that she had arrived, and both Cheryl and the secretary heard Mr. Young say that it was all right for her to come into his office. The secretary, after motioning Cheryl toward the office, turned her back to Cheryl and began typing.

"Cheryl said, for a few moments, she hesitated outside of the office door. When she walked in, he was sitting in a large chair, facing the window, his back turned to her. She said she shut the door, but he did not turn around. When she began talking about what she was remembering, he sat perfectly still. She felt the anger well up inside of her when she saw that he was ignoring her. She called his name, but he said nothing, and he did not face her.

"Suddenly, she said, she was five years old again and Harold Young, her friend, was pushing her down on the ground. She was kicking and screaming, but he was strong. She tried to bite him, but he slapped her on the face; she felt the sting from the blow. She was looking into his eyes, and the friendliness had been replaced with a frightening glare. He was saying things that didn't make any sense to her. She was crying, begging. She was scared, helpless, sick. Her head pounded, her stomach churned; she was vomiting.

"The next thing she knew, she said, she was pulling out the gun and shooting Young through the chair several times. Evidence showed she shot three bullets through the chair. Harold Young's secretary and four other people in the nearby offices came running into the room.

"Cheryl dropped the gun and fell to the floor on her knees, where she was found crying when the police arrived.

"The reports from the coroner and the ballistics expert show that Young died of gunshot wounds inflicted by the gun that had Cheryl's fingerprints all over the handle."

"Why?" Mama asked, as if thinking to herself. "Why?"

"Why what?" I said.

"Why didn't he talk to her on the phone?"

"I don't know," I answered. "Maybe he didn't have anything to say to her."

"Then why did he tell his secretary to make the one o'clock appointment?"

I shook my head.

"And why didn't he turn around and look her in the face when she walked into his office?"

"I don't know," I said. "The only person who really knows the answer to those questions is Harold Young, and he is dead, remember? Anyway, Cheryl shot the man. She admits it; five witnesses saw it. What we've got to do is to try to verify the rape account. Mr. Jacoby wants a verdict of voluntary manslaughter."

"Why?" Daddy asked, pushing through the apartment door. I had given him a key and he had used it.

"Voluntary manslaughter is killing in the heat of passion after being provoked," I said.

"Sounds like murder to me," he said.

"Trust me, Daddy, it's not murder. Anyway, with that verdict, Mr. Jacoby can make a plea for a reduced sentence. I have *got* to find out if Cheryl was raped by Harold Young, and I have *got* to do it soon. Hopefully Mr. Jacoby can convince a jury that Harold Young had provided, through the rape, adequate provocation."

"That's ridiculous," Daddy said. "How can you prove that the man provoked somebody to kill him through something that he had done over twenty-five years before?"

"Mr. Jacoby doesn't have to prove it," I said. "He just has to plant the seed of reasonable doubt in the jury's mind. If there is any doubt, no matter how slim, it can't convict her.

"That's stupid," Daddy said. While we talked, Mama sat quietly, her eyes indicating that something was going around in her head; something wasn't sitting right with her and I knew it. The telephone rang. I answered it. It was Cliff.

"Do we want Cliff to bring wine for dinner tonight?" I asked.

"What?" Mama responded, her mind obviously not on dinner, or any meal for that matter.

I sighed. "You might want to bring some beer," I said. "Daddy likes Miller." After a few more brief exchanges, I hung up the phone.

"Mama," I said, interrupting her thoughts. "We are having company for dinner tonight. We can pick this up first thing in the morning."

She nodded absently as she stood up and walked toward the kitchen. "I can't understand why Harold Young *would not* talk to Cheryl over the telephone."

After that, neither Cheryl's nor Young's name entered the conversation again that night.

Cliff arrived around 5:30 P.M. with two cases of Miller Highlight, a bottle of Johnny Walker Red, and several bottles of Asti Spumante. "They're not alcoholics," I whispered cheerfully.

He grinned. "You said they'll be here for three days," he said. "I don't expect them to drink it all tonight."

When we walked into the kitchen, our senses were tantalized with the smell of fried chicken mingling with the odors from the pots of food that covered the stove and oven. As usual, Mama appeared genteel when she greeted Cliff, but Daddy didn't pull it off so naturally. He eyed Cliff suspiciously, and when he finally spoke, his voice was so choked that whatever he mumbled was inaudible.

"Is the beer cold?" Mama asked, pointing to the stack of liquor that Cliff had put on the kitchen table.

Cliff nodded nervously.

"James, why don't you pop a beer?" Mama suggested. "It'll be another hour before supper is ready."

Cliff picked up the hint, reached and popped a can, then handed it to my father. Daddy reached for the beer and took a long sip. "Mmmm," he finally said when the can came down from his mouth, "it is good and cold."

Cliff smiled, popped a can for himself, and took a long swallow. And thus the ritual was over. Daddy smiled and said, "You've kept the Honda running smoothly." He took another gulp of beer. "I appreciate you taking good care of my little girl's car. Since I'm so far away, it's good to know that there's somebody who can help her whenever she has car trouble."

"My father is a mechanic," Cliff said, his shoulders relaxing noticeably. "I grew up either fixing, washing, or waxing cars."

"Really," Daddy said, gulping down a swallow of beer and putting his hand around Cliff's shoulders. He led Cliff toward the living room. "It's kind of a hobby with me. I just mess around with cars," he said. "You know, enough to keep our vehicles running pretty good."

"Well," Cliff wisely said, "keeping a car running is what a good mechanic is all about."

Daddy agreed, and when they had exited the kitchen, Mama smiled. "He's nice," she said nonchalantly.

"He is," I smiled. "Really, Mama, he's a nice guy. He's not perfect like Daddy, but...."

Mama raised her eyebrow. "Honey, your father hasn't been perfect since the day *before* we got married."

We laughed.

"What I mean is that you and Daddy seem to have a lot going together," I said. "All these years, you've still got things clicking between you."

"Most of the time," Mama admitted. "Simone, the secret of successfully living with a man is to accept him for what he is; no matter what, don't try to change him! If what you see is not exactly what you expected to get, accept him anyway and always insist that he accept you. It takes a couple of years before you get to that point in a marriage, but once you both are satisfied that whatever you've got in each other is all that the other person can give, the rest is a piece of cake."

"I can't believe you've never tried to change Daddy." I commented.

"I tried, but it was both frustrating and fruitless. I thought about it and decided that I could live with the things about him that I didn't particularly like."

"Such as?"

"Such as his evasiveness, his constant complaining about having to fix our cars, his determination to live in Hampton, and the numerous other ticks that use to drive me insane...."

"Mama, he's not that bad," I said defensively.

She laughed softly. "No, he's not that bad, but he could be if I didn't accept those aspects of his personality."

"I guess I understand what you mean," I said.

"Are there things about Cliff that you're literally crazy about?"

I nodded. "For the most part he's great, but still I'm not sure."

"Take my advice and wait until you're *absolutely* sure. Once you make up your mind that he's the guy for you, buy into him completely—lock, stock, and barrel. Remember, whatever you buy, it belong to you.... You own it completely."

"Sounds ominous," I said.

She smiled. "If Cliff becomes the permanent mister in your life, accept him for what he is.... For God sake, don't waste your time trying to change him!"

"I won't," I said as our heads turned toward the roar of laughter coming from the living room. "They seem to have hit it off nicely."

Mama nodded introspectively. "Now, I'll have to keep things warm for another forty-five minutes. It'll take that long before James' beer has kicked in and he will have mellowed out."

The doorbell rang. I answered it, welcoming Donna and Ernest into our little party.

"Cliff, get Ernest a beer," Daddy ordered, after I had introduced him to Daddy. "And bring me another one; I've just about knocked this one off."

Cliff obeyed and followed Donna and me into the kitchen. He winked as he took three beers out of the refrigerator. After he'd returned to the living room, I turned to Donna and said melodramatically. "Donna, I want you to meet my mama," I threw my hands out, "a living, breathing Miss Marple."

Donna smiled, a little embarrassed.

"Well, Donna," Mama said sweetly, "it's good to meet you. I've heard a lot about you."

"Really?" Donna said sheepishly.

"Let me assure you," Mama said, "they were *all* good things."

Donna's eyes perked up. "Oh, and I've heard good things about you too, Mrs. Covington," she said.

Mama's voice was reassuring. "Call me 'Candi,'" Mama said.

Donna's face relaxed. "Simone has told me a lot of nice things about you, Miss Candi," Donna said in her usual hurried manner.

"Well," Mama said, changing the subject, "I hope you enjoy the spread of soul food we've fixed today.

We've got candied sweet potatoes, fried chicken, bar-becued ribs, potato salad, macaroni and cheese, rice, fried okra, carrots, and...."

"My goodness," Donna interrupted. "Who are we having to dinner?"

"Mama and Daddy will be here three days," I said. "We're not cooking anymore after today, are we, mother?"

"No," she agreed readily. "We've got other fish to fry the rest of my time here. Sit down, Donna. Do you drink beer?"

Donna nodded.

"Then get one out of the refrigerator. We've got another thirty minutes before we call the men in to eat. Meanwhile," she said looking at me, "let's put the dishes and silverware on the table."

Thirty minutes later, the six of us were digging into the feast that Mama had almost singlehandedly prepared.

"Candi is the best cook around," Daddy was saying, his mouth full of fried chicken.

"I'm a convert," Cliff added, agreeing. Ernest nodded approvingly, his mouth so full of food that he couldn't speak.

"Simone," Donna asked, "can *you* cook like this?"

"I refuse to answer," I said, getting a fork full of Mama's fried okra and rice, "on the grounds that it might incriminate me."

Chapter 12

Sunday, September 3

The food and the alcohol pretty much confined Daddy to bed for the better part of the next day. We had wisely given him the only bedroom, and when I peeked in, I saw that he had spread out in the bed, lying on his back, with his mouth open, ragged snores jerking out as he inhaled, puffy short breaths as he exhaled.

He had really enjoyed himself the night before…. It was almost two in the morning when Ernest, Cliff, and Donna finally left to go home. Every time they would attempt to leave, Daddy would insist that they have something else to eat or drink. He told some of his raunchy army jokes and they laughed as if they genuinely enjoyed listening to that stuff. Several times, he asked them somewhat personal questions, but they good-naturedly answered him without any embarrassment.

A few times, very few times, Mama interrupted and changed the subject, but all in all she allowed the evening to flow naturally. I made the comment to Mama that I'd never seen Daddy enjoy his own sons as much as he seemed to enjoy talking to Ernest and Cliff. She agreed but added nothing to my observation. I looked at her kind face and wondered why she could never interact with her sons the way she does with other people. Strange, I thought, that she's never said anything negative or positive about their relationship.

Because Mama insisted that the kitchen be spotless, it was after 3:00 A.M. when she and I finally opened the couch in the living room and fell into bed. I was too tired to take a bath, almost too tired to undress. I managed to take my clothes off before falling into the pull-out bed, and it was eleven o'clock the next morning when I awoke, a bit foggy.

I took a long hot bath and brushed my teeth. I drank several cups of coffee before I felt fresh and alert for a conversation with Mama. I pulled the black leather armchair by the window where I could see the sun streak through the tall trees that flanked my apartment building.

"There *is* one thing I haven't told you yet," I said, feeling proud of what I was about to reveal. "Harold Young's birth was recorded as a girl."

"What?" Mama asked, interested.

"It found out when I began checking the courthouse records. It was at the Bureau of Vital Statistics that I found a copy of Harold Young's birth certificate and it showed that he was a girl."

"What was his name?"

"Henrietta Young."

111

"How do you know it's the same person?"

"It took a while to track it down, but it's the same person. Both the birth certificates of his sister Charlotte and Harold, or should I say Henrietta, listed the same parents. There was no child born as Harold Young."

"What happened?"

"An amendment to the original birth certificate was made just before Harold entered school. It was the amendment that showed that the child was a boy and his name was changed to Harold."

Mama frowned.

"I wonder whether that's significant," I commented.

"I don't know," Mama said. "It's something to keep in mind. Anything else?" she asked.

"I talked to Mary Lawfton, the cleaning woman who worked in Young's office building. She told me that, while Young seemed like a nice man, she knew for a fact that he was a sex pervert."

"What does she mean?"

"I don't know exactly. Said she had evidence though."

"What kind of evidence?"

"She said that while he was in his office every night, she knew for a fact that he wasn't exactly working."

"What did she mean?"

"I don't know," I admitted. "She wouldn't say any more to me about it. Said she didn't want to lose her job.... Said she had five children to support."

"She probably wanted you to offer her money," Mama said.

"Money. I couldn't offer her money," I said. "After all, I'm not a private investigator. I'm used to getting information from public sources, where you don't have to grease anybody's palm for legitimate information."

"She's doesn't know or care about that. She's probably thinking you're like the detectives she sees on television. Anyway, try to get her phone number. This is the Labor Day weekend, she's probably not working tomorrow. I'm not like you. I have no aversion to greasing her palms if she's got proof that the man had a propensity toward sexual perversion."

Since I'm accustomed to using public records to track down information, it was frustrating for me to try to find Mary Lawfton's phone number. It was Sunday, everything was closed, and the next day wouldn't be any better. It would be a holiday, so I finally resorted to calling Mr. Jacoby at his home. He graciously talked to Mama for about twenty minutes, then promised to call us back with the number.

Daddy woke around four o'clock, took a shower, and decided to take a walk. Cliff called around five, saying that he had eaten and drunk so much the night before he was heading to the gym to try to work some of his gluttony off. Daddy came back around six, drank a cup of coffee, and went back to bed.

Donna called about 6:30 P.M. to ask Mama's suggestion on what to give Ernest for intestinal pains. Mama talked to her and suggested some kind of antacid.

Since neither she nor I wanted to look at food for a while, we both spent the day drinking water, trying to move some of that soul food within our stomachs. Feasts like the one we had enjoyed the day before were good, we both agreed, only when they were followed by a few days of famine.

True to his word, Mr. Jacoby called us around 7:00

113

P.M. with the telephone number. It took several tries before we actually talked to Mary Lawfton. The first time we called, a man with a sober voice told us that she wasn't home.

The next time we called, a child said that she was in the bathroom. It was on the third attempt that she answered the phone herself. When I asked her to meet with Mama and me, she was reluctant. She hemmed and hawed for several minutes. Finally, I put Mama on the phone and listened as she subtly hinted that there was money to be had if Mary would talk to us in strict confidence.

Miraculously, Mary agreed to seeing us at her house the next morning around eleven o'clock.

Mama hung up the phone and picked up a stack of papers. She drew a breath and smiled at me with genuine pleasure. "Simone," she said, "I'm going to be perfectly honest with you. I don't think Cheryl killed Mr. Young, and I want you to help me prove it."

I sat back down in the armchair by the window without saying a word. Cheryl had walked into Harold Young's office and shot him five times in the back. She hadn't tried to run away; the police had found her on the scene of the crime the exact time that they discovered the body. Cheryl's fingerprints were all over the gun; it was her gun; and it was positively identified as the weapon that had fired the fatal shot. There were five eyewitnesses who had gone into the office immediately after the shooting and had seen Cheryl with the gun, and more importantly, Cheryl had confessed to killing the man.

I looked at my mother intently. "Mama," I said, trying not to sound too irritated, "what possible reason can you have for believing that Cheryl didn't kill him?"

Mama looked at me seriously, her eyes filled with warmth. "There are several things that don't make sense to me," she said patiently. "First, why did Harold Young not speak to Cheryl over the telephone? Second, why didn't he turn around when she was standing in his office with a gun to his back?"

I threw my head back and laughed. "Mama, that's something only the dead man knows," I said.

"But we have to find out," she said, her voice urgent. "The answers to those two questions will solve this mystery."

I listened to Mama skeptically. "What mystery?" I asked, "The fact is that Cheryl pulled the trigger to a gun she purchased, and the bullets from that gun entered Harold's body and killed him. Look at the coroner's report," I said, pointing to the stack of papers she had just pulled together. "Look at the forensic report."

"I know what the reports say," she countered. "Think, Simone. If somebody told you that they remembered your raping them twenty-five years ago, wouldn't you turn around and try to talk about the incident? We have to find out why he didn't turn around."

I stood up enthusiastically. "I don't know, Mama," I said. "But I do know that Young was alive a few minutes before Cheryl fired the bullets in his back. Remember, both she and the secretary swore that it was his voice they heard saying it was all right for Cheryl to enter his office. And, there is absolutely no door other than the one that Cheryl entered.

"If someone had left by the window, it was virtually impossible for them to avoid being seen by people on the street. Remember, this happened about one o'clock in the afternoon. It was lunchtime, in the down-town area; the streets were literally crowded. Somebody would have noticed a person out on a window ledge...."

Mama was shaking her head. "Relax," she said. "Take it easy. I'm not saying that somebody killed Harold a few minutes before Cheryl went into his office and then crawled out on the window ledge. That's not what I had in mind at all."

I slumped back into the seat. I was exhausted; my head was spinning. I was really trying to follow Mama's logic, but I just couldn't understand what she was suggesting. "Then what?" I asked.

"Try to dismiss the fact that Cheryl shot the man in the back," Mama said. "Just suppose Cheryl walked into Harold's office, began talking about the rape, and then turned and walked out again. What would be the purpose of having her come to his office?"

I shook my head. "I don't know."

"Remember," Mama continued. "Mr. Young was the one who set the appointment.... He was the one who told Cheryl to come into his office. Why would he want her to come in and talk to his back and then walk out again?"

I took a deep breath. "It doesn't make sense," I said.

"Exactly," she said. "It doesn't make sense; it would have been pointless. Now, think about the ordeal from Harold Young's point of view. He had realized that Cheryl had vague recollections of him during their trip to the Bahamas. Several months later he gets a phone call from her, and he refuses to talk to her over the phone.

"But he *does*...," and Mama emphasized the word

'does' by lingering on it for what seemed a full minute, "tell his secretary to make an appointment with her for one o'clock that same day.

"When Cheryl arrives, he tells his secretary to send her in, but when Cheryl walks into his office, he never says a word and never turns around to look her in the face. He literally sits there, without moving a muscle, and allows Cheryl to shoot him in the back. That just doesn't make sense, now does it?"

I had to agree with her, but I couldn't think of a reasonable explanation. "What do you propose we do?" I asked submissively.

"We need to think beyond whether Harold Young was a sexual pervert or not.... We need to find out more information about him, about his motives, his actions."

"You've got something specific in mind?" I asked.

She shook her head. "Tomorrow, when I talk to Mary Lawton, I'm going to ask her to do something that you might find offensive, but believe me, I think it's absolutely necessary in order to save Cheryl from years of imprisonment."

"What?" I asked.

"I'm going to offer Mary Lawton money to allow me to go into Harold Young's former office and search it. Since she is the cleaning woman, she's probably got a set of master keys."

"You mean you're going to enter his office illegally. I suppose you know that any information you might find this way can't be used by Mr. Jacoby in court?"

Mama nodded. "Yes. If I find something that he needs, I'll leave it untouched. You can tell him about it and he can get it legally, or do whatever he thinks best. Right now, I've got to find out why Young did

117

not talk to Cheryl over the telephone and why he did
not turn around when he knew she was holding a gun
to his back."

"Maybe he didn't know."

"Maybe he didn't care."

Chapter 13

Monday, September 4
Labor Day

It was six o'clock when I awoke, and I lay in the soft bed for a while. For the moment, I reveled in the rest, trying to reconstruct Mama's theory. Although my gut feeling told me that Cheryl had not killed Harold Young, I couldn't get past the fact that she had actually shot him.

My feelings aside, the mechanical aspects of the crime were clear. The coroner had ruled death by gunshot wounds, gunshots from Cheryl's gun. Mama's reasoning that if Cheryl hadn't shot Young there wouldn't have been a murder didn't make sense. If there hadn't been a murder, she wouldn't be Mr. Jacoby's client and I wouldn't find the whole thing confusing. I lay there, my mind trying to remember a dream, a dream that held a clue to the mystery, but somehow I couldn't grab hold of it.

I got up and folded the bed back into the couch. Now that Daddy was back to normal, Mama had returned to sleeping in the bedroom with him. I took a bath, soaking uninterruptedly for fifteen minutes, trying to figure out Mama's reasoning.

By seven o'clock, both Daddy and Mama were out of bed. I smelled the percolator, so I wasn't surprised to see them sitting at the kitchen table drinking coffee and eating toast.

"What's for breakfast?" I asked.

"We're still fasting," Mama said quietly.

Daddy smiled. "I don't want to see food again for at least another few days," he said.

"I'm finished with the bathroom," I said. Daddy took his turn next, bathing and shaving while Mama moved around the apartment quietly, speaking only to answer Daddy's questions. I knew she was thinking; I'd seen her like this many times before. It always amazed me that Daddy never seemed to notice how her mood changed whenever she was involved in a mystery.

This morning he asked, "Where are my socks?" Later he wanted to know, "Did you bring my after-shave lotion?"

Daddy began pacing up and down the apartment like a trapped animal. "I thought I would get to see some of this town before I go back to Hampton," he said.

I got up from my chair, went to the end of the table where he was sitting, and kissed him. "I can't take you around today," I said. "Mama and I have plans. Tomorrow, I'll spent some time with you."

"I'll tag along with you and your mama," Daddy said. "I don't mind looking into the stores."

"We're not exactly going shopping," I said, trying to figure out a way to keep him busy for a few hours while Mama and I kept our appointment with Mary Lawfton. "Wait a minute. I'll call Cliff and see if he'll be willing to take you to see the town."

I walked over to the phone and dialed Cliff's number. It took six rings before Cliff picked up the phone. "Cliff, this is your favorite person calling," I said, since Daddy was standing right next to the phone, breathing down my neck.

"Favorite person," Cliff said. "You're more than my favorite person."

"Be that as it may," I answered, solemnly.

"Oh," Cliff said, catching my hint. "And how are you and your wonderful parents doing?"

"Mama and I are doing just fine," I said, my voice relaxing, "but Daddy is bored.... He wants somebody to play with."

Daddy grimaced. "No I don't," he snapped.

"What did he have in mind?"

"I don't think he has anything particular in mind," I said. "He just doesn't have anything to do. Mama and I are going to run an errand. We'll be back around two o'clock, and that's the time they plan to leave to head back to Hampton. Until then, Daddy is at loose ends. Got any suggestions?"

"Give me an hour to shower and shave. I'll pick him up at nine."

"Thanks," I said. "I owe you one."

"You'll pay me," he said devilishly. "You can count on it."

I hung up the phone and told Daddy that Cliff would pick him up in an hour. His face brightened perceptibly. Mama smiled absently and kept moving quietly throughout the apartment, picking things up, dusting them and putting them back down in the exact same place that they had been. I knew she was thinking about Harold Young, Cheryl, and now Mary Lawfton.

When Cliff picked Daddy up, Mama remained quiet and reserved, giving Cliff an innocent glance when he walked into the apartment.

"What's the matter?" Cliff whispered.

"I'll explain later," I said. "You and Daddy have a good time."

He nodded, gave me the handsome grin that made my insides stir, then motioned Daddy, who had been standing by the window watching for his arrival, toward the door.

We had two hours before our appointment, so I suggested we ride around town for a while. Mama agreed, but as we drove downtown and I pointed out prominent places, Mama seemed uninterested. The traffic lights went through their programmed changes, but hardly a car passed; there were very few pedestrians. Mama was quiet until I pulled my Honda up in front of the address Mary Lawfton had given us.

Mary Lawfton lived in a tenement house on Ashburn street, not far from downtown Atlanta. I knocked on a rattling blue door that swung inward into a dimly lit vestibule. A young man, every bit of twenty, opened the door and invited us into a long corridor that ran the length of the house. The only light in the entryway came from a tiny window facing the stairs. The dimness obscured the color of the paint. The boy led us to the left into a kitchen in the back, where we met Mrs. Mary Lawfton.

I was aware of the countertop and the old-style sink filled with dirty dishes. The stove and refrigerator were old, as were several small appliances set against unpainted walls. She pointed at two kitchen chairs and chased several children out the back door.

"Now, missy," she said, wiping her hands on a dirty apron. Her stomach fell down toward the floor and the apron hung loosely over a dirty blue house dress. "What can I do for you?"

Mama fixed her eyes on Mary's eyes and smiled sweetly. "I've got a few dollars," she said, "to prove to my daughter that what you said about Harold Young being a sex pervert is true."

Mary Lawfton's expression softened a bit. "It's true," she said. "I'm not twisting the truth."

"I've been around a long time," Mama said, becoming more serious. "I know what these men who stay shut up in their offices do. My daughter doesn't believe me, but I told her that I'll give you fifty dollars...."

"Wait one minute," Mary said, springing up from the chair and leaving the room in haste. Mama winked an eye and opened her purse. In a few minutes, Mary returned carrying six or seven magazines. She handed a few to me and the others to Mama."

"Wouldn't you say it would have to be a sex pervert to read these kinds of magazines?" she asked, her face frowning.

I felt my eyebrows raise as I flipped through the pages of the magazines she had handed me. There, in color and black and white were graphic pictures of children being sexually abused in every conceivable way. I took a deep breath and tried to break a smile as I closed the pages.

"It's child pornography," I said, staring uneasily.

Mama flipped through a few pages, then closed the magazines abruptly. "And you swear you got these magazines from Mr. Young's office?" she asked.

Mary flashed a twisted smile. "Them and plenty more," she said. "You won't believe how many of those magazines I threw away..., bunches of them. He didn't even try to hide them; he threw them into his wastebasket every night and watched the disgusted expressions on our faces when we looked at him. He seemed normal enough, but he was a *pervert*, I tell you. My sister's boy, the one who answered the door, worked with me one night and he brought those few home with him. I'd never bring anything like that in my house. I'm trying to raise five kids and...."

"Why did you keep these copies?" Mama asked.

"I didn't know they were here until that crazy woman killed Mr. Young. My sister's boy figured somebody would be asking questions about Mr. Young, so I thought it was a good idea to keep a few of the magazines, in case somebody was willing to pay...."

Mama opened her wallet, took out two twenties and one ten-dollar bill. She handed them to Mary, who snatched the bills from her hands eagerly. "I'd like to buy these magazines," Mama said. "This is strictly a business deal."

"That's fine with me," Mary said, biting her lower lip. "Like I said, I'm trying to raise five kids."

"Tell me, Mary," Mama continued, her voice serious. "Is there anything else?"

Mary looked down at the money. She reached into her pocket and pulled out a sheet of paper, then handed it to Mama.

Mama looked at the paper, frowned, and handed it to me.

"Mary," Mama said. "I've got some more money that I'm interested in investing, if you know what I mean."

Mary smiled. "I know exactly what you mean, and I'm listening," she said.

"I'd like to get a look around Mr. Young's old office," Mama said. "Just to satisfy my curiosity, you know."

"I know how it is when your curiosity needs satisfying," Mary said. "Anything I can do to help?"

"Well, I'd like to get my hands on a key to that office."

"Missy," Mary said, "this being the holiday and all, I had to turn the master key back in to the office. I won't have another chance on getting that key until tomorrow night. Of course, it'll be expensive to get a key made from the master key. I could lose my job and all and I've got five kids...."

"I know," Mama said. "How much you think it'll cost?"

"Couple hundred dollars," Mary said, squinting her eyes. "Like I said, I could lose my job if somebody used that key to steal something."

"Let me tell you what I can do," Mama said. "Tomorrow afternoon my daughter and I will return here with a hundred dollars. On Tuesday afternoon we'll return and pick up a copy of the key to Mr. Young's office. After we test the key to make sure it's the right one, we'll return and give you another hundred dollars and the matter will be closed. What do you think about that?"

"I think you've got a deal," Mary said, grinning. "Of

125

course, if anybody asks where you happened to get such a key, I won't know nothing about it. After all, I'm not the only cleaning woman in the building using that master key."

"I understand," Mama said.

"Any one of ten other cleaning women could have made you a key, and if anything gets stolen...."

"Don't worry," Mama said reassuringly. "I'm not going to take anything from the office. I just want to inspect it, that's all. I promise you nothing, *absolutely nothing* will be removed from that office by me or anybody else using that key."

"I believe you, missy," Mary said, looking down at the fifty dollars she held in her hand.

"Is that office occupied now?" Mama asked.

"Yes, missy, two or three people done been in that office since Mr. Young got killed. I really don't think you'll find too much of his stuff in there anymore. We cleaned the place through and through before the first man moved in there."

"Did you change any of the furniture?" Mama asked.

"The chair that he got killed in," Mary answered. "They replaced it with a brand new chair."

"Naturally," Mama said. "But what about the desk or bookcases or any of the other furniture."

"No, missy, they didn't replace that stuff. That furniture is good stuff. They weren't about to get rid of it just because it happened to be in the room where a man got himself killed."

Mama breathed deeply, then rose. "Mary, you're a good woman to do business with," she said. I stood up. Mary motioned us back down the dark hall toward the front door.

126

"Now, I can expect you back here tomorrow night with a hundred dollars?" she asked.

We nodded. "If you have the key. As soon as I get an opportunity to make sure it works, I'll come back and give you the other hundred," Mama promised.

"You've got a deal," she said, first shaking my hand and then Mama's. "I don't know what two black women care about Harold Young getting himself killed, but for two hundred and fifty dollars I don't rightly care," she said, shutting the door behind us.

Chapter 14

Tuesday, September 5

My mother and I were trapped in my bedroom, the tiny upstairs room of an old farmhouse. Down below dogs barked and snapped as they hunted us. The dogs' barking grew to an ear-splitting roar, drowning out my screams.

"I'm going back to Hampton!" Daddy shouted.

I sat up in the bed, my heart pounding. It was six o'clock in the morning and I was trembling from the dream's insistent realism.

"You can spend your vacation here running around Atlanta with Simone if you want to, but I've got things back home to do," Daddy continued.

I pulled down my nightshirt and walked toward the bedroom. Daddy was standing in the bedroom doorway, leaning on the door frame.

"That's a good idea," Mama said, looking directly

into his eyes. She drew a breath. "You've got things to do in Hampton, and I've got things to do here. Actually, I prefer to spend my vacation here instead of in Hampton."

"You're not going back with me?" Daddy asked, his lower lip starting to tremble.

Mama held her head high and kept a straight face. "No, I'm not," she said, turning her back to him and walking over to look out of the bedroom window.

He stared at her for a moment or two. "You're not going to spend your whole vacation running around Atlanta with Simone, are you?" he asked.

Mama turned to face him and smiled. I felt the tension relieved. She took a step toward Daddy. "James," she explained quietly, "there are a few things I want to do here. As soon as I finish, I'll come home."

Daddy's face was full of anguish. "I'm not coming back to get you," he persisted.

She glanced from him to me. "Simone will bring me home," she said softly.

"Simone's got a job," Daddy said, his anger diminishing. "She can't be running you up and down the road."

Mama hesitated. "Then I'll take the bus; don't worry," she said thoughtfully. "You go back to Hampton and do the things you'd planned to do. As soon as I get finished, I'll come home. I promise."

Daddy raised an eyebrow. "Candi, you need to go back to Hampton with me now," Daddy pressed.

"I can't," Mama countered.

Daddy made an irritated gesture. "What do you mean, you can't go home? That's ridiculous. You mean you don't *want* to go home now."

"James," Mama said. "I'm helping Simone research something for her boss. We're pretty close to getting to the bottom of some sticky business. I promise you that this matter will be cleared up completely in the next few days.... No later than a week; I promise. After it's all over, I'll come home and I won't be coming back to Atlanta for a long time."

"You promise?" Daddy asked.

She walked over and kissed him on the lips. "James, I promise. This thing is almost over. When I come home, I'll tell you how it ended."

Daddy looked at me for a moment, as if he was embarrassed for his anger, then flashed a familiar charming smile. He walked over and kissed me. "You take care of your mama," he said. "Bring her home when she's finished. Don't put her on a bus."

"I won't," I promised.

Daddy walked over and hugged Mama, then released her. "Pack my things," he muttered. "I'll go down and check the car. I'll be back in a few minutes." A half hour later, in the pouring rain, he was headed back to South Carolina, leaving Mama and me with the freedom to solve our mystery.

Several hours later, the rain hadn't let up. "What do you think about the note Mary gave us?" I asked.

"I don't know," Mama said.

"I have to turn it over to Mr. Jacoby," I said.

Mama nodded.

The note that Mary had given us was torn from Harold Young's desk calendar. It showed that Cheryl definitely had a 1:00 P.M. appointment.

"He was expecting her," Mama whispered.

Later, she and I made a dash to the Honda, getting

damp despite our umbrellas. Mama was unusually quiet. Driving around the winding curves and slick hilly roads demanded my full attention, so I wasn't obliged to interrupt her thoughts with small talk. There were few cars out on the highway, and after a while I relaxed. Without conversation, the beating of the rain on the windshield became hypnotic. Suddenly, the screech of tires and the long, indignant blare of a horn told me that I had run a red light. I pulled over and took a deep breath. Mama smiled and glanced at her watch. After a few minutes, I cautiously edged back out into traffic.

It was a little after one o'clock when we were finally seated in Sidney Jacoby's office. Mama's mood had completely changed. She was quite garrulous now, telling him about her theory and why she suspected that Cheryl had not killed Harold Young.

"It's just an uneasy feeling," she said. "Something about Mr. Young that makes me think there's more to his death than meets the eye."

Mr. Jacoby listened quietly, refraining from interrupting with any questions. His only movements were a slight nod that caused dandruff, like snowflakes, to shower the shoulders of his navy blue suit and a slight twitch near his right eye.

"I suppose what I'm saying," Mama finished up her argument, "is that for some reason Harold Young didn't act like a man who was afraid of being hurt or killed," she said.

Mr. Jacoby rose and walked to the large window at the rear of his office and stood with his back to us, looking out. The rain had slowed to a drizzle. For a full five minutes, he stood silently contemplating. Finally he turned back to us and said, "Suppose he wanted her to kill him. What would have been his motive?"

Mama shook her head. "I really don't know," she said. "I've heard nothing to justify Mr. Young's setting Cheryl up to kill him, but I can't get it out of my mind that he had made an appointment to see Cheryl and then refused to acknowledge her presence."

He sat down, picked up a pencil, and began tapping it on a yellow legal pad that lay before him on his polished desk.

"Well," Mama went on, her manner totally composed, "Simone and I have made a proposition with a...."

"Don't tell him about it," I interrupted.

Sidney Jacoby's eyebrows raised as he considered us carefully. "If it's illegal," he said slowly, "I don't want to know anything about it."

"We need two hundred and fifty dollars," Mama said politely.

"Out-of-pocket expenses," I grinned, laying a finger against my nose.

"I'll authorize you to get it from petty cash," he said, looking at me warily. "I suppose you can't get a receipt."

"No," I said, shaking my head.

"No matter," he sighed. "I'll get something to show on the books."

Feeling pleased with herself, Mama pushed further. "I would like to make a request," Mama said, adding, "if you don't mind."

Mr. Jacoby opened his hands. "What?"

"I'd like for you to arrange for Simone and me to pick up Mr. Young's desk calendar from his office tomorrow morning."

"No problem, but suppose they don't have his desk calendar?" Mr. Jacoby said. "Then what?"

"Simone and I need to obtain something from that office tomorrow. It would be nice if it could be his desk calendar, but we need to be at that office sometime in the morning."

Mr. Jacoby took a deep breath, then broke out in a smile. "I hope you two are not getting in over your heads," he said. "Remember, you're not the police."

"We're all right," I said with assurance. "So far, we're only following a hunch."

"A hunch," Mama said, "that nobody else has even thought of, so our actions shouldn't provoke suspicion."

Mr. Jacoby straightened slightly. "That's a very good point," he said.

The rain had slackened to a drizzle, which made the drive a bit easier, but I still drove ten miles under the speed limit. After all, I was in no hurry. Mama was quiet again, but this time she had a look of contentment on her face. As I drove I reflected on how I thought this was going to be such a simple case. I should have known, I said to myself, that Mama would have seen something beyond the obvious. I pulled up to Mary Lawfton's house, jumped out, and rang the doorbell. She came to the door and hurriedly gave us the key, practically snatching the hundred-dollar bill out of my hands. "You'll be back tomorrow night with the other hundred?" she asked.

I nodded.

"And you ain't going to steal nothing from that office?"

"Nothing will be taken from the office," I said, trying to reassure her with one of Mama's smiles. "You've got our word."

Mary flashed a short grin, then shut the door.

We stopped by a Burger King and picked up a couple of hamburgers to take back to the apartment. Mama had sent most of the food back home with Daddy, so there weren't many leftovers. The phone was ringing as I started undoing the upper of the two locks on my door. I heard it ring five times, but by the time I got the bottom lock open and sprinted across the hall to the living room, the caller had hung up. The light on the answering machine was flashing. Mama took the bag of hamburgers to the kitchen as I flipped on the answering machine to hear the messages. The first was from Cliff; he would call back later. Donna had called, inviting me and Mama out to dinner.

I looked up as Mama walked back out of the kitchen. She was shaking her head. "Not tonight," she said. I agreed.

The last message was from my father. "Candi and Simone, I've gotten home safely," Daddy said. "Everything at the house is fine.

Mama nodded and walked back into the kitchen. I followed her to put on a pot of coffee.

"Is Cliff coming over?" Mama asked, sitting down at the table and pulling hamburgers from the white and red bag.

I reached up into the cabinet and took out two cups. "He's leaving for Chicago early in the morning. He doesn't expect to return until the weekend."

"What's he working on?"

"A divorce case," I said, "a nasty one."

Mama shuddered.

I smiled devilishly. "Don't you think you would enjoy the intrigue of tracking down an adulterer?" I asked.

Mama shook her head implacably. "I don't think so," she said. "There's something ugly about getting between a married couple."

"Well, don't feel alone," I said. "Cliff doesn't like it either. As a matter of fact, this case is really getting to him. He doesn't even want to talk about it. I must admit it has made him look at our relationship a little more seriously."

"In this divorce case Cliff is working on, are there children involved?" she asked.

"From the little I can gather, there are," I acknowledged. "But as I said, Cliff doesn't talk about it much, so I don't know the details."

There was a hint of a smile on Mama's face; her eyes widened.

"What the matter now?" I asked.

"I wonder why Mr. Young never fathered children?" she mused.

"Maybe *she* was unable to have children."

"I don't think so," she said. "Something in Mrs. Young's manner makes me think she may have refused to have them."

"You think she knew about her husband's molesting children?"

"You remember how, when we visited her, she didn't seem to be particularly grieved that her husband was dead? At the time, it surprised me that she was even willing to talk to us, knowing that your boss was representing the woman accused of killing her husband."

"I admit," I said, pouring the freshly brewed coffee, "it seemed strange that she still spoke fondly of Cheryl."

Mama smiled impishly, and I could see that she was deducing again. "Just maybe, if I visit her alone, she'll tell me a little more about the late Mr. Harold Young."

I pouted. "You mean you don't want me to go back with you?"

"Not this time. I think I can get more out of her if I go alone. She might want to tell somebody about her husband, somebody who will listen and understand."

I shrugged my shoulders; I was in no mood to argue. I took a sip of the hot coffee and bit into my hamburger.

Chapter 15

I don't know how Mr. Jacoby pulled it off, but somebody in Harold Young's old office found a cardboard box of miscellaneous items that had been removed from his desk after he was killed. Yes, it included his desk calendar, and it would be possible for two of Mr. Jacoby's employees to pick up the box of his effects, since it was simply sitting in a storage room, collecting dust. Mrs. Young had been contacted, and she had given her permission for the attorney to have the articles.

Mr. Jacoby assured us that his request had aroused no suspicions. It seemed to everyone to be obvious that Cheryl was guilty of murder and the case would be cut-and-dried, so the request for the desk calendar was treated routinely.

Mama made it clear that the real reason we were

going to the office was to make sure the key Mary Lawfton had given us would get us into the office that Harold Young had occupied. Once we ascertained that it worked, we were going to go back to Mary Lawfton to pay her the other hundred dollars.

Mama's plan was to engage the receptionist in a conversation. Then, when she gave a signal, I would go to the office and try out the key. Of course, we had to make sure that office was empty first. That part, Mama said, we'd play by ear.

Things were getting exciting, I thought. In the past, I had spent weeks digging up information that Mr. Jacoby needed, but I'd never had an experience such as this one.

When we drove up to the headquarters of J. Higgins & Sons, clothier, I couldn't help whispering, "The game's afoot." Mama smiled.

We left the car in the paid garage among rows of others and walked underground until we reached the front door of the basement of the building.

The Higgins company headquarters occupied the first ten floors in a twenty-five-story building on the southwest side of Bankhead Avenue. Its curved, aquatinted glass sides represent the newest trend in Atlanta architecture. The elevator banks had been built around a small jungle of trees and creeping vines.

As soon as we exited the elevator on the third floor of the building, we saw Cindy sitting in a swivel chair behind a wide desk in front of the bank of six elevators. Mr. Jacoby had given us her name as the person who would turn the box over to us. To her left was a word processor and a telephone with about twenty lines.

Cindy was a short woman, with a jolly red face that flushed even redder when she laughed. She had blue eyes that lighted up when she talked. She liked people; she was an extrovert with an eager smile and a quick tongue.

"So you've got a new boss," Mama said without making any introductions.

"I can't say that I like Mr. Samuel better than I did Mr. Young," Cindy said without any prompting. You wouldn't have known that she had never met either of us before this moment. "He's not as nice, although I must admit he's more professional, you know."

Mama forged right ahead. "Oh," she said, with a tinge of surprise in her voice, "I guess it's hard to beat Mr. Young, since he was such a nice man to work for...."

"If you ask me, he was sick," Cindy said. "Not well."

Mama raised her eyebrow.

"What was the matter?" she asked.

"Don't know," she said.

"Was he sick the day Cheryl came to the office?" Mama asked.

"Don't know," she said.

"What makes you think he was sick?" Mama asked.

"The way he looked, the way he talked."

"Did he ever say he didn't feel well?"

"Never said much of anything," she replied. Cindy sat with her hands in her lap, the green cursor of her word processing blinking on a blank screen in front of her.

"Why?" Mama asked.

"I don't know," she said. "I worked for him over five years, and he was always the last to go home."

She winked. "We thought he might have been impotent. We all, I mean the secretaries that is, talked about him and wondered what kind of woman his wife was to put up with a man who wouldn't come home after a day's work."

"His work load might have...."

Cindy waved her hand in disgust and shook her head. "His work load wasn't that heavy," she said. "I remember looking in his office and seeing him comb through maps of the city. He seemed to be writing down information about Lord knows what."

"Did he give you things to type?"

"Sometimes, but he never gave me any of the notes he'd made, if that's what you mean." Cindy paused. "To be honest, Mr. Young was a man of very little activity." She smiled. "He didn't produce much results either. There were few letters or reports to type."

Mama asked, probing, "What *did* you do for him?"

"Not much," she said. "Months would go by and he'd stay locked up in his office all day and I would sit out here, bored to death. The company pays me a good salary; I didn't want to lose my job, so I finally volunteered to help the other secretaries. After a while, I became known as the overflow secretary."

"The what?" Mama asked, surprised.

"The overflow secretary.... You know, whenever other secretaries had too much work or deadlines, I'd take care of their overflow. It was better than sitting here doing nothing, and I still got paid as an executive secretary."

"Do you have that problem with your new boss, Mr. Samuel?" I asked.

"Not him!" Cindy said. "He gets out in the field, so

140

I have to prepare his travel and expense accounts. And he sends out letters, memos, prepares reports. He does all the things an executive vice president gets paid big bucks to do."

Mama shrugged. "Well, all I can say for Harold Young is, if the company paid him big bucks to do nothing, he wasn't doing too badly."

"I suppose," Cindy said. "That is, if you like getting paid big bucks for doing nothing. That's not my style."

"Exactly what kind of person was Harold Young?" Mama asked. "I mean, what kind of personality did he have?"

"He was nice. Most people liked him. There were times when he was hyper-aggressive," Cindy said, "running around as if the place was on fire."

She smiled and added, "I'm taking this class in psychology, and I'd say that Harold Young was a Type A personality. You know, even though he never got much done around here, he was running and pushing. Most people liked him, but oddly they stayed away from him. On the outside, he appeared hard-driving, but nobody could understand why he never produced much of anything. I've never seen a man so busy, and yet, to be perfectly honest, I'm surprised he kept his job."

She leaned over and whispered, "Sometimes, I used to think that he had something over the heads of the powers that be around here and they were a little afraid of him."

"Did he have *any* friends?" Mama asked.

"Everybody liked Mr. Young. He was warm, friendly, and most of the time easy to talk to, but nobody could get inside of him...or his office for that matter. He never went out to lunch. Every day, the boy from the restaurant would bring him the same lunch—hamburgers, french fries, and coffee. He'd sit in his office, prowling through maps, writing long notes, and eating alone."

At that moment, a tall black man walked out of a nearby office. "Cindy," he said. "I'm going out for a while. If I get any calls, I'll be back in a hour."

"Yes, Mr. Samuel," Cindy said cheerfully.

Mama took a deep breath as she watched Mr. Samuel step on the elevator. "I'd like to get the box with the effects of Mr. Young's office, please. Mr. Sidney Jacoby called and said you'd allow us to pick it up."

Cindy sighed, stood up, and walked down the hall toward a closed door. "I was wondering when you two would finally tell me what you wanted," she mumbled. Mama gave me the signal, and I stepped back toward the door that Mr. Samuel had just exited and tried the key that Mary had given us. It worked. I breathed a heavy sigh of relief and stepped back to the desk about the same time that Mama and Cindy returned with a small cardboard box.

"I'm surprised Mrs. Young didn't get these things," Mama said, picking up the dust-coated pencils, pads, scotch tape, and such.

"In all my years of working here," Cindy said, "she's never come to this office."

"Not even when he was killed?"

She shook her head. "I tell you I've never seen the woman. I don't know if she's ever called him on the phone, but I can tell you that I've never actually had a conversation with her."

"Cindy," Mama said, smiling graciously, "out of curiosity, did Mr. Young have any relatives or close friends that you knew of?"

"He had a sister," she said. "Charlotte Young."

"Did you ever meet her?"

"Of course not. She called a few times, and when Mr. Young was in the bathroom, I took a message. She said she was his sister."

"Anybody else call him often?" Mama asked.

"Why do you want to know?" Cindy asked abruptly.

Mama flashed an innocent smile. "It just beats me," she said, "that this woman Cheryl, the one who shot Harold Young, you know...."

Cindy's expression softened. The phone rang and she answered it. When she hung up the phone, Mama continued talking to her as she wrote out a message and put it down on her desk. "It just beats me that she didn't try to get close enough to shoot him earlier. A crazy woman like that...."

"If she tried before, I never knew it," Cindy said, shuffling the several pink pads on her desk. She called that morning. I guess you read about that in the papers."

Mama nodded. "Other than that," Cindy volunteered, her face twisting in thought, "I don't know of her ever calling him. The only people who called occasionally were his sister, his wife, and his doctor."

I moved down the hall. "Where are you going?" Cindy asked, looking at me closely.

"I was trying to find the bathroom," I said nonchalantly.

"You're going the wrong way," she said, pointing. "It's at the other end of the hall."

I walked toward the bathroom as Mama picked up the desk calendar from among the pens and pencils that

143

were in the small box. By the time I came out of the bathroom, Mama had pushed for the elevator and was thanking Cindy for her time. Cindy, on the other hand, was trying to tell Mama about Mr. Samuel's trip away from the office. He was really going to the barber to get a haircut; he did that kind of thing on company time, but she'd never tell his boss.

Mama smiled and nodded; then we both jumped on the elevator and waved goodbye to Cindy through the closing doors.

"Thank goodness that's over," Mama said. "Does the key fit?"

"Perfectly," I said.

"I guess that means we owe Mary Lawfton another hundred dollars."

"Learn anything new from chatterbox Cindy?" I asked.

"A few things, but first let's go by and give Mary her money. I want to come to work with her tonight. Then I want to call Mrs. Young to see if I can visit her in the morning, and then...."

"Wait a minute," I said. "Slow down."

"I want you to take this calendar," Mama said, decidedly more slowly, "and go through it meticulously."

"What am I looking for?" I asked.

"I only flipped the pages," she said. "It's not filled with appointments, but I noticed a few names and circled dates. See if there are any connections."

"Okay," I said. "I'll do that."

"Good," Mama said. "Our three-day fast is over. Let's find a restaurant and eat; I'm starved."

Chapter 16

Wednesday, September 6

Mama and I sat in the Honda, waiting for the office cleaners to come to work. An old woman with carefully dyed hair came walking slowly down the sidewalk on the other side of the street. Moving up briskly behind her was a pale teenager with brown hair cut short, frizzed around his head in a perm, and wearing designer jeans. I held my breath, sensing trouble.

The old woman turned and glared at the boy. "What do you want?" she growled, her voice loud and deep.

The boy shrugged. "Nothing, lady, nothing," he said, and hurried past her. I exhaled.

"I just knew he was going to mug her," I said to Mama.

"Why?" she asked innocently.

"Did you see the way he walked up to her?" I asked. "He probably did intend to grab her bag, but she wasn't an easy prey," Mama said, smiling. "Did you see that look she gave him? Like, you better not even try it!"

I agreed. "I guess, in the city, you can't be afraid to live."

The fall coolness had already begun setting in, and despite the light of the clear blue sky at six o'clock, in another half hour I knew that dusk would cover the city. I felt somewhat uneasy and asked Mama again about our plans.

"I've persuaded Mary to let us walk into the building along with the other workers," she said.

"What if the night watchman asks Mary to identify us since he's never seen us before?" I asked.

"Mary flatly refuses to get involved. She's not going to prevent us from walking in with them, but if we're challenged, we're on our own. I suppose we can't blame her for being too careful...."

Before Mama finished her sentence, the cleaning service mini bus drove up and went down into the underground parking lot of the office building, and I swung my Honda in behind it, parking alongside it. About six people jumped out of the van, along with Mary, all absolutely refusing to look either Mama or me in the face.

They were wearing ordinary street clothes except for uniform shirts that identified their cleaning company. Mary casually nodded toward the backseat of the van, where two extra shirts lay. She turned her head and walked a short distance as Mama and I put on the shirts, then picked up some of the rags, pails, and sponges like the other workers were carrying. We fell into step behind the group of workers going upstairs. Together the nine of us marched into the building.

There was a night watchman on duty, a tired old white man whose face was filled with tiny wrinkles. He looked up at us impassively, not saying anything. He didn't blink or move his head, just glanced at us through expressionless brown eyes, then turned back to reading his magazine. Mary pushed the button for the elevator, and when it arrived the nine of us got on. Mary pressed the button for the tenth floor. The other workers looked down at the floor, deliberately ignoring Mama and me. The only sound we heard was the humming of the elevator moving up through its shaft. It stopped on the tenth floor, and all the other workers hurriedly got off and scattered in different directions.

Mama smiled, then nudged me toward the stairs.

The stairs were dark; there wasn't even a safety light. I shuddered; I am nyctophobic. Ever since I was a child, I had been afraid of dark places. Whenever I go into a room at night, I reach in and hit the light switch first. I had never outgrown that fear, and Mama knew it. She pulled out a small blue flashlight that I'd seen in Daddy's tool box, switched it on, and shined it around.

She grabbed my hand. "Take it easy," she whispered. I almost attached myself to her warm body, and with the sound of my heart pounding in my chest, we inched down the seven flights of stairs to the third floor.

I could hardly stand the five minutes it took us to walk down in the pitch darkness, with only the one small ray of light from the flashlight. I held Mama's arm so tightly she moaned.

"Am I hurting you?" I asked.

"Yes," she replied, a note of pain in her voice. "Your

nails are digging into my flesh!"

"I'm sorry," I said. But in fact I couldn't release the pressure on Mama's arm until she opened the door into the third-floor reception area. I took a deep breath and glanced at my watch. It was about seven o'clock. In the reception area where we had talked to Cindy earlier that day, no windows opened to the outside. It was completely dark. I felt myself shiver. Using Mama's flashlight, we picked our way past Cindy's desk.

"Suppose the security guard visits each floor?" I asked.

"I don't know. We'll just have to listen for him," Mama replied.

We moved to the office that had formerly been Harold Young's. As we expected, it was locked. It took a couple of minutes of fumbling in the dark with the little flashlight before Mama found the key to open the door. The office door was solid wood, so we didn't have to worry about light shining through a panel. Closing it softly, Mama flipped a switch and we took our bearings.

This was a real office. The furniture was made out of real wood, walnut. Thick gray carpeting covered the floor. An antique clock stood against the wall facing the desk. A view of the parking lot was mercifully shrouded by heavy drapes. I peeped through the drapes; the sun was going down. We put our pails down and slipped on rubber gloves.

"What are we looking for?" I asked.

"I don't know," Mama said. "But I've got a hunch that Harold Young was doing some sort of work of his own in this office, spending ten to twelve hours a day in here. His secretary said he was always looking over maps and writing down information."

"If he left notes or personal papers of some sort, don't you think they would have been in that box we got this afternoon?" I asked.

"No way. He would have kept them hidden, and I believe they're still in this office."

We worked as quickly as we could. The file cabinet wasn't locked, so I picked a couple of files from a few manila folders. Nothing in them indicated that they had anything to do with Harold Young. I handled the pages carefully, making sure to leave them in their original order, then I refiled them neatly.

"You'd think he was some kind of secret agent," I said.

"That's it," Mama said, her eyes shining. "Look for a secret drawer, compartment, or safe, that sort of thing."

Mama tackled the desk. She began fumbling with the lock, it was open. "Nothing in here except a half-empty bottle of Scotch and a few empty prescription bottles," Mama said. She shook her head as she flipped through a stack of sports magazines. Then she got down on her hands and knees and crawled under the large desk. After a few minutes, she crawled back out again.

"Nothing under there," she said.

My heart was beating fast. "I've examined the file cabinet," I said. "There's nothing in them."

"Check the credenza," Mama instructed.

After a few minutes, I was satisfied that there was no hidden drawer inside of the credenza.

Mama pulled out a chair and sat down. She closed her eyes in bewilderment. I sat quietly on the floor, one leg under the other. In my line of sight was the beautiful clock facing the desk. I thought about examining it but decided against it. It was so small, nothing could possibly be hidden inside of it, I thought.

Mama sat quietly; finally she opened her eyes.

"Is there a safe?" she asked.

I got up and examined the walls, looking behind pictures. There was no safe.

"I guess the only place we haven't looked is behind the clock," Mama commented.

"That thing is so compact," I said, "there is no way anything could be hidden inside of it."

"It's the only thing that's left to examine," she said. She got up out of the chair and walked over to the clock, then tried to move it with one hand; it would not budge. She tried pushing it with two hands. It still wouldn't move. She leaned up against it; her 140 pounds wouldn't even shift it.

"Come here," she said. "Help me move this thing."

Together we pushed the clock; it still wouldn't budge.

Mama was obviously surprised. "It doesn't *look* heavy," she said.

She reached back into her pail, pulled out her flashlight, and squatted down on the floor, examining the base of the clock.

"Look," she said.

I joined her. It was obvious that the front of the clock had a panel that had been replaced. Despite the fact that it fit snugly, it was not original and not the work of a professional cabinet maker. Mama tried to push her fingernail inside the panel, but it was clear that it would take more than a fingernail to pry it open.

"Your curiosity is getting the best of you," I whis-

150

pered. "The panel probably came apart and somebody glued it back..., somebody who wasn't a carpenter."

"I don't think so," Mama answered. "There's more to it than that. There might be a catch somewhere that will open this thing. Look for a spring," she ordered.

"You've been watching too many old movies," I said. "Somebody would have to be a real craftsman to rig up something like that."

"Maybe not," Mama said, trying to maintain her composure. She put her back against the clock and tried to move it again. It was unmovable. She took a deep breath. "The base is thick enough and wide enough to have a compartment the right size to keep papers inside," she said.

"What kind of papers?" I asked. I couldn't find a catch, and I wasn't convinced that there was one.

"Papers like maps and pads with lots of notes written on them. Harold Young's work that he never got typed, edited, or printed, remember? For a man who worked so hard making notes and writing stuff down, why weren't there any papers found in his office upon his death? And why did he make sure nobody came into his office?"

I failed to see her point. "You think he was working on some kind of book?" I asked.

"I've just got a hunch that there is more to Harold Young than meets the eye!"

We heard footsteps coming down the hallway, along with the rattling of keys.

"It's the night watchman," Mama said, jumping up and flipping off the light switch. We both stood perfectly still in the darkness, listening to the footsteps, which hesitated outside the office door. Finally they

151

moved down the hall.

"What are we going to do now?" I whispered, feeling unprepared to go to jail for breaking into an office that yielded absolutely nothing but suspicion that the base of a clock might have a secret compartment. After several minutes, we heard the voices of the cleaning crew.

"What's happening, Charlie?" we heard a young man say.

"Everything's quiet," the night watchman drawled.

We heard the guard and cleaning man walk away. Mama counted slowly to one hundred and then opened the office door. The reception area was empty, but we could hear the cleaning man whistling in an office farther down the hall.

"Let's go," Mama whispered. "Mr. Jacoby will have to get somebody in here to open that thing."

"Sounds good to me," I said. "If there is evidence that we need to take out of here, we'll have to get it legally if it's to be used in court."

"I know," Mama smiled, her shoulders relaxing. "You've told me that often enough."

Ten minutes later we were down the stairs and on the first floor. Mama cracked the outer door. The guard had made it back downstairs and was sitting at his station, directly facing the front door. After a few moments, one of the cleaners joined him, and we watched as they talked. Mama closed the door.

We had to get out. Mama decided to go up one flight of stairs to the second floor. I followed her. We went into the reception area, and she used the receptionist's telephone to call downstairs to the guard.

"This the night watchman," she said in broken

English. She listened for an answer. "Listen," she said after a few moments. "It looks like somebody been up in this office before I got here. If anything missing, I ain't took it."

Mama listened to the guard's reply.

"I'm on the eighth floor," Mama continued. "You better come up here and take a look."

She hung up the phone and smiled deviously. We went back down the stairs and opened the outer door again. The old night watchman and the cleaning man he'd been talking to were getting onto the elevator. The door closed, and Mama and I slipped through the lobby and out the side door.

We stripped ourselves of the cleaning shirts and jumped into the Honda. "We'll have to give these shirts back to Mary," I said.

Chapter 17

Thursday, September 7

Thursday morning, it was after nine o'clock before I first peeked at the light of day. It was cloudy. Even though the torrential rains had ended, the sun refused to show its face.

Now that Daddy had gone home, I was back in the comfort of my own bed, at least half of it. I stretched, inching my legs as far as I thought I could without touching Mama.

She was not in the bed.

My first impulse was to jump up and find her, but I resisted it. I needed the solace of being alone. I lay thinking how my mama had endowed me with keen vision and a quick mind, yet I couldn't figure out where she was going with the murder—yes murder, I repeated—of Harold Young. Why in heaven's name was she so interested in Young's personality, his job, and his wife? Why couldn't the scenario simply be that an emotionally dysfunctional woman walked into a man's office and shot him to death? Why couldn't this be a simple case of trying to prove that Cheryl should be given some consideration because of an experience that left her emotional scarred? And for that matter, I thought, what information did we have that Cheryl was emotionally scarred? She had been under psychiatric care for nine years; so what? We still hadn't found any evidence to support her allegation that Young had molested her.

I rolled over in the bed, gripped my pillow, and squeezed it.

Mama was on to something, I thought. But what? What could get her so fired up that she was treating Harold Young like the criminal and not Cheryl?

"What is Mama seeing in this case that I can't see?" I grunted.

"What did you say?" Mama asked, pushing through the bedroom door. She had a nice little tray that somebody had given me for some obscure occasion. On the tray were two cups of coffee and a plate of toast, eggs, grits, and bacon.

"I was saying that I love how you look when you cook me breakfast and serve me in bed," I teased.

"Cut the bull," Mama said. Then she set the tray down on the bed in front of me. "You were asking," she said as if she had bionic ears, "what I see in this case that you don't."

"My words exactly," I said. "Tell me why is this case turning around in the opposite direction?"

Mama put the tray on the nightstand next to my bed. I picked up a cup of coffee, put in two packets of Equal, and began stirring it slightly.

"I'm sorry," Mama said methodically, picking up the other cup and following the same routine, "but I don't see Harold Young as an innocent victim."

"What gives you the idea that his death was not...?" Mama interrupted. "I first felt like something was wrong when I talked to Mrs. Young. I got the feeling that she was deliberately trying to convey that there was something questionable about her husband's character. Most wives attempt to present their husbands in a favorable light. That's why I want to talk to her again, this time alone," she said.

She took a deep breath, then continued. "Anyway, the things that everybody—Mrs. Young, Cheryl, Mary Lawfton, and his secretary—are saying about Mr. Young give me a strong feeling that he *wasn't* killed."

"What things?" I asked.

"You know, just things they said, certain words, or their attitudes, innuendos, things like that. I tell you, Simone, there is a secret in Harold Young's life that will throw more light on this matter, and I'm not going to stop until I find it!"

"For God sake," I said impatiently, "if Cheryl didn't kill the man, then who killed him, and how?"

Mama frowned, and her eyes became teary. "I don't know yet," she said, her voice soft. "I think I've got an idea of what happened, but at this point I can't be sure."

I felt like a traitor; I had forgotten the only rule to our game. After all, I had asked for her help, and she was there for me. I had invited her to Atlanta to go with me to talk to Mrs. Young; now I needed to reciprocate by giving her my wholehearted support. I knew that her abilities were astute.

I lowered my head and, putting my cup down on the tray and picking up my plate, I changed the subject. "This is delicious," I said after swallowing several mouthfuls of food. "Candi," I teased, imitating Daddy's voice and mannerisms, "you've outdone yourself again."

Mama stood up and, with her cup in her hand, walked over to the window. "God," she said introspectively, "I wish this thing made sense to me. There's got to be something in the base of that clock that will prove my theory."

"What do you expect to find in the clock?" I asked.

"Papers. Maps. Notes. Maybe a diary. Whatever it was that Harold Young was meticulously working on for years in his office."

I finished off my grits and eggs. "Well, we'd better hop to it. What do you want me to do now?" I asked, picking up my half empty cup.

"I want you to take the desk calendar and go through it with a fine tooth comb. As I said yesterday, I didn't see many names in it, but I want to know if there was anybody that he talked to or scheduled to talk to more than twice."

"And," I teased, trying to lighten up her mood, "what are *you* going to do, Miss Marple?"

"I've already called Mrs. Young to ask to visit, but she can't see me until tomorrow. Isn't it odd that she consents to talk to me? I really think there's something she wants to tell somebody."

"Well, if she's got something to say, you'll get it out of her," I said. "What are you going to do while I laboriously comb through this challenging desk calendar?"

I asked.

"I'm going to stay in the apartment, do some cleaning, scrubbing, things like that."

"Are you saying that my apartment needs cleaning?"

"I can't believe that refrigerator!"

"Well, cleaning it is on top of my 'to do' list," I lied. She began laughing hard, throwing back her head. "Yeah, and I've got some ocean property in Arizona to sell you," she joked.

"Give me a break," I said. "What about the base of the clock?" I asked. "We need to call Mr. Jacoby to see if we can get it open to find out if there is anything inside."

"I've already talked to him this morning. Fortunately, he got into the office early," she said. "He's somewhat skeptical about there being something important there, without our giving him concrete evidence. But I persuaded him to get a court order to go into the office and open the clock."

Mama's voice dropped, her mood changed. "He made it clear to me that the judge will have his tail if they find nothing there."

At that moment, I felt sorry for Mama. I sighed. "We may be going too far out on a limb with this one," I said, "since all you've got going is a hunch."

"It's more than a hunch," she continued. "My heart knows I'm right, but my head doesn't understand why. Perhaps tomorrow, after I talk to Irene Young, I'll have something to confirm my feelings."

She was right; I could see it in her eyes. "I'm with you all the way," I whispered.

Mama's brow wrinkled. "I tell you, Simone, I feel that I've had a revelation," she continued. "Like a psychic experience. It's kind of frightening. You know, in the past, whenever I've had a hunch, I would always be able to substantiate my judgment with some kind of evidence or documentation. This time I'm going down alone; the only thing I've got going for me is my intuition."

I could see that Mama's confidence was at stake, and I thought, reflectively, so is Cheryl's life. "Whatever happens," I said reassuringly, "Simone is here; I'll always be here for you."

The telephone rang; I reached over and answered it. It was Cliff. I smiled girlishly, and Mama yawned, then walked out of the bedroom. After half an hour of talking with Cliff, I hung up the phone, picked up the tray, and walked to the kitchen. Mama was stepping out of the bathroom, wrapped in a red bath sheet.

"You're next." She smiled, going into the bedroom.

I went into the bathroom, ran the spotless bathtub full of water, poured a generous amount of Avon Skin So Soft bath oil into the tub, and eased down in the hot water to soak for the next half hour.

I could hear Mama in the kitchen, washing dishes, pots, and pans. It's therapy for her, I told myself selfishly.

It was eleven o'clock when I finally got down to looking through Harold Young's desk calendar. Mama was cleaning the refrigerator, something that I seldom accomplished.

"His secretary was right," I said, raising my voice so that she could hear me in the kitchen. My apartment was rather large, but with a little effort I could communicate from the living room to the kitchen. "There's nothing much here. Mr. Young didn't do too many things, or if he did he didn't note them down on his calendar."

"Is there anybody he talked to more than twice?" Mama asked.

"His doctor," I answered.

There was silence for a few moments; then Mama walked gingerly out of the kitchen into the living room and flopped down in the black leather chair across from the couch. "That's it!" she said triumphantly.

"That's what?" I asked.

"Get Mr. Jacoby on the phone while I put these plastic gloves back into the kitchen," she said.

"You have to use plastic gloves to clean my refrigerator?" I asked, dialing my boss' telephone number.

She nodded. "I don't know what you've got growing in there," she said.

When she came back into the living room, I was talking to Mr. Jacoby. I handed Mama the telephone.

"Mr. Jacoby," she said sweetly. "Simone and I have been examining Harold Young's desk calendar, and it seems that he had been seeing a doctor...."

"Dr. White," I said. "Dr. Kelvin White."

"Dr. White," Mama repeated. "Dr. Kelvin White. It seems that he had been seeing Dr. Kelvin White a number of times...."

I hurriedly flipped through the book. "Six times in the last few months of his life," I said.

"Six times in a few months," Mama repeated. "Is it possible...?" Her tone took on a subservient twang. "For you to find out exactly what he was being treated for?"

Mama listened for several minutes. "Thank you," she said with a little more confidence in her voice.

160

"Yes. We'll let you know if anything else surfaces."

She turned to put the telephone back onto the receiver. "Mr. Jacoby said to tell you he'll expect a full written report of everything we've been doing the past week," she said.

"He didn't have to tell me that," I said.

Chapter 18

Friday, September 8

The next morning when I woke up, Mama was standing by the window with her back facing the bed. My mother, whose salt and pepper hair is worn in a short layered cut, was wearing a pair of tailored, chocolate colored slacks, a yellow blouse, and a pair of brown two-inch-heel sling-back shoes. I studied her silently for a few moments, wondering what was going on in her mind, trying to comprehend the special intuition she possessed that had made her question facts that no one else had challenged.

I glanced over to look at the nightstand; there was no tray, no breakfast in bed.

Mama heard me stir and turned toward the bed. I could see determination in her eyes, a demand to be believed. "I want to go home today," she said calmly.

"Why?" I asked groggily.

"After I've had my chat with Mrs. Young, there's nothing more that I can do here. I need to go home to be with James."

"You can't go home today," I said. "Donna and I haven't had a chance to show you our little secret places."

"Your what?"

"Our secret places in Lennox Mall. You know, the where-you-shop-till-you-drop boutiques."

Mama stretched and yawned. "I'm ready to go home," she said, lifting her hands in a gesture of frustration. "I need to put some distance between me and this problem."

"I'll make a deal with you," I said, swinging my feet around to the edge of the bed. "If you stay today, I'll get Donna to get up early in the morning and go with me to drive you back home. That way, I can do the driving on the way there and Donna can do the driving back, so the trip won't be so hard to take in one day."

Mama sighed; her brows drew together.

"Take it easy," I said sympathetically. "Things will work out. I'm sure Mr. Jacoby will find something in the base of that clock...."

A little embarrassed, she raised her eyebrows. "I'll treat you to breakfast," she said, her mood lightening.

"Sounds good to me," I said, jumping out of bed and jogging toward the bathroom.

"After breakfast," Mama said as I closed the bathroom door, "you can drop me at Mrs. Young's."

"You're going shopping with Donna and me, aren't you?" I yelled over the steaming shower.

I thought I heard Mama mumble, "Uh-huh."

A half hour later I had on a pair of jeans and a

favorite T-shirt. I was stringing up my Reeboks.

"You're dressing comfortably," Mama said. She was sitting in the black leather chair, watching me run from the bathroom to the bedroom, trying to get dressed.

"We're going to shop till we drop," I reminded her, feeling the glow of excitement I always get when I'm about to spend money. "You'd better find yourself a pair of walking shoes."

She got slowly to her feet, picked up a pair of soft shoes, and put them in a bag near her purse. "I'll leave them in the car," she said. "And I'll put them on *after* my visit with Mrs. Young."

"How long do you plan to spend with her?" I asked.

"About an hour," she said. "After you drop me at her house, wait a full hour before coming back for me. That'll be about as much time as I need."

Half an hour later, we were at the Pancake House ordering pancakes with butter and a big order of bacon. We lingered over breakfast as long as we could. At ten o'clock, I dropped Mama off at Mrs. Young's.

I drove back north to the Trust Company of Georgia bank. I went into the underground parking lot, which was almost full. I whistled under my breath as I took the elevator to the first floor of the bank. I needed money to shop, and neither my checking account nor my charge cards could stand the strain. I had to go into my nest egg to withdraw a couple of hundred dollars. My favorite banker, a flirt named Josh, kept me occupied a full twenty minutes before I could get back down to the parking lot.

Next I headed for the post office. I needed stamps and I had to pick up a week's worth of mail. It was the wrong time of day to go to the post office; there was a fifteen minute wait in line. I threw my mail onto the backseat of the car. It would be another three days before I looked at it again.

The dry cleaner I frequented wasn't very close to my house. In fact, it was almost across Atlanta, but I'd gotten to know the owner when I had done some research on another case. The old black guy was so helpful that I had got in the habit of taking my clothes to him, and his prices were right. No matter how long I stayed away, he was always glad to see me.

Midday is not the best time to drive in Atlanta, and it was exactly an hour later that I began heading back to pick Mama up from in front of the immaculate lawn that framed Mrs. Young's house.

"How did it go?" I asked.

Mama was smiling. "Sufficient to say," she said, "that I'm onto something big—something bigger than I'd ever imagined."

My jaws dropped slightly. "What?" I asked.

Mama looked at me majestically and rubbed her arm. "After Mr. Jacoby examines the clock, I'll tell you all about it," she said. "If the evidence isn't in the base of that clock, it's somewhere in that office, and we'll have to tear it apart until we find it."

"My goodness, Mama," I insisted a little too forcefully. "What did she tell you?"

Mama stared at me disdainfully.

"I'm sorry," I said as politely as I could. "I just want to know what you know. We're partners, remember?"

Mama's voice was bright, confident. "She told me everything that I suspected and more," she said. She leaned back in the seat of the car and put the seatbelt over her shoulder. "Now, let's go shopping."

I slumped over the wheel, totally frustrated. I leaned back in the seat. "And to think," I said, turning on the engine of the Honda, "that just this morning I was feeling sorry for you because you were frightened that your hunch might not work out."

"I've never been frightened," Mama said.

"You certainly weren't overconfident," I said.

"Which direction are we heading?" Mama asked, totally ignoring my words and taking off her high-heeled shoes. She slipped on a pair of flats.

I glanced in her direction. "We're going to Lennox Mall," I replied. "What are you in the market for?"

"Shoes," Mama said. "Lots and lots of shoes."

I inched my way downtown and eased off the expressway. The mall was not crowded; parking was easy.

We shopped for the next few hours. At five o'clock Donna joined us at LaPeep, where we ate dinner. After putting our bags in the car, we went off to another wing in the mall. We had money that had to be spent.

Chapter 19

Tuesday, September 19

"I stopped by Sheriff Abe's office a few days ago," Mama said. "He's worried about the Jones boy."

I was sitting in Mama's kitchen, finishing off a piece of apple pie and a glass of juice. "You mean the son of that Reverend Jones whom nobody seems to be able to flush out of the woods?" I asked, looking up at her.

She rolled her eyes. "The same one," she replied.

"What's the matter with the boy?"

"You know he's living with Miss Peterson."

"Miss Sally Peterson who lives on Highway 601 outside of Nixville?"

Mama nodded. "She's a foster parent. There were no other children in her home right now, so DSS felt it was all right for him to live there. Abe asked me to visit her, and I stopped by and talked to her yesterday."

"And?"

"Even though the boy goes to therapy five days a week, I've got second thoughts about him."

"Did you see him?"

"Briefly," she said. "Sally told me the only time he comes up from the woods is when it's time for him to go to therapy. For a while, he wouldn't even come up for that, but Sally told the sheriff, and Abe came out and threatened to lock the boy up if he didn't keep his appointments."

"What else did Sally tell you?"

"She said that he still wets the bed."

"That big boy? He's at least sixteen! He's still wetting the bed?"

"That's still not all Sally told me."

"What else?"

"He has set seven fires in her bedroom."

"You're kidding!"

Mama shook her head. "I wish I were."

"He might need to be locked up."

"Sally said he's paranoid about being confined." Mama took a deep breath, and I could see compassion in her face. "I suppose we shouldn't be surprised that something is wrong with the boy."

I shrugged. "I guess if I had a father as evil as the Reverend Jones, I'd be weird too."

Mama was sweeping the floor when suddenly she stopped, leaned her chin on the end of the broomstick, and stroked the handle with one hand. "You remember when we found the dead child?" she asked absently, as if she really didn't expect or want an answer.

I nodded.

"That's the first time I felt it!"

"Felt what?"

"Something evil. I remember…." She continued staring thoughtfully. "I was looking into the boy's face."

I thought for a moment. "It was when that bear of a man appeared at the edge of the woods," I said.

Mama put the broom back in the closet. "No," she said. "I remember looking directly in the boy's eyes." She sat down at the other end of the kitchen table.

"Some time ago," Mama said, "I asked you to look up some information about men who sexually molest children, remember?"

"Yes," I said.

"What did you find out?"

"Most child molesters were themselves molested when they were children."

"Then it's a learned process?" Mama asked.

"Yes," I answered, "a cycle. The abused becomes the abuser."

"Are sexual molesters murderers?"

"Some, but not all. Why?"

"I didn't tell you the other thing Sally told me."

"What?"

"The boy has gradually killed every one of Sally's cats!"

"All of them?"

"He hung them on the clothesline, one after the other. Sally said she almost died with grief, but he made her promise not to tell the sheriff about it."

"Is Sally scared of him?" I asked.

"I think so." Suddenly Mama's mouth gaped open. "And maybe she should be. After all, he might be a killer," she said.

"Aren't you exaggerating?"

"I don't think so. It's something I sense," she said,

"when I look into his face, into his eyes. All along, we thought that Reverend Jones was our killer because Rita told me that he had molested his daughter. Yet few people would verify the accusation, and the folks who talked to me didn't believe that the Reverend would kill. If that is true, then we have to look for another killer, and the boy would fit the bill. Think. If Reverend Jones had molested the boy, the son might be imitating his father. Miss Aggie could have told the boy that Rita was going to find evidence to put his father away, and since he knew that he had been doing the same thing as his father, he might fear that he too would be put away. So he killed both Aunt Aggie and Rita."

"Why kill his mother?"

"She might have found out and told him she was going to have him put away."

"Why would he kill his sister?"

"The girl had been sexually mutilated. He probably went too far, that's all."

"That's a lot of conjecture," I said.

"Maybe so, but we'll have plenty time to look for evidence *after* we get that boy out of Sally's house. Mama picked up the phone and called the sheriff's office. When she hung up, she grabbed the keys for her car and headed for the door. "Abe will meet us at Sally's house," she said.

It was two o'clock in the afternoon when we left Mama's house. The ride to 601 normally takes about a half hour, but Mama made it in fifteen minutes. I was about to complain when we pulled up into Sally's yard. Sally's house sits back off the road about a quarter of a mile. That evening, the only thing odd about the place was that there were no cats. Sally Peterson's love for

170

felines is known throughout Hampton and Jasper counties.

We parked the car and walked the twenty feet to the edge of the porch. At first there was no sound from the house. However, when we stepped onto the porch we heard a low noise that sounded like growling.

We looked through the window.

The boy had Sally backed into the corner, his right hand on her throat, his fingers digging deeply into her neck. His body was twisted so that we could see his face. His eyebrows were arched, his eyes glowing with insanity. The remainder of his face was as impassive as a block of wood.

"Old woman," he was saying, "you told the sheriff I killed your cats! You want me locked up…!"

"No, no!" Sally begged, her voice barely audible. She was trying to grab his hands, but he laughed at her and applied more pressure.

"Please…." Her voice was a whisper. "Please…."

For a moment we stared in disbelief. Then Mama grabbed my hand and stepped back from the window. "Sally!" she called out as loudly as she could. There was no reply. "Sally!" Mama called again. "It's me, Candi. I've talked to Sheriff Abe about the boy, and he's coming…!"

At that moment, we heard the thump of Sally's body as it hit the floor. A few seconds later, the back screen door slammed shut.

"He's probably going into the woods," Mama said, reaching for the front screen door.

When Sally came to, she coughed and gasped for breath through her bruised throat.

"He's gone," Mama said softly. "It's all right now."

"He was trying to kill me," Sally said, her voice caught between anger and dismay.

I stood wiping the sweat from my face.

Mama stroked Sally's hair. "I know," she said, her voice calm and serene. "But it's all right now."

"He was going to kill me because he thought I planned to have him locked up."

I glanced at my watch as Mama looked up. Sheriff Abe stepped through the doorway.

"We know who your killer is," Mama said enthusiastically, "and if you hurry, you'll find him in the woods behind this house."

Two hours later, Abe had dogs and helicopters combing the woods behind Sally's house. Early the following morning the Jones boy was captured and locked up.

Chapter 20

Wednesday, December 6

The trial in the case of *The State of Georgia vs. Cheryl LaFlamme* had been going on for two days, Judge Frank Henderson presiding. Mr. Jacoby always wanted to know as much as possible about any judge he would be appearing before, so I had fully researched Judge Henderson's background and opinions in other murder cases. I had found that the judge was generally considered to be a fair man, but he was not regarded as one of the most brilliant legal minds on the bench.

Mr. Jacoby was pleased.

The first two days was spent hearing the prosecution's case, which had gone as expected. There was no new evidence. To the prosecutor, it was a simple case of Cheryl LaFlamme willfully and deliberately, with malice aforethought, going to Harold Young's office, shooting, and killing him.

The district attorney's most important witnesses were the five people who had gone into Harold Young's office immediately after hearing the shots. After a few minutes of cross-examination, however, none of them were sure of how much time had passed between the time Cheryl had gone into the office and they heard the three shots. They had rushed into the office, and they had all seen the same thing: the gun was on the floor and Cheryl was standing there.

It was obvious, according to the prosecutor, that Cheryl was a menace to society and she should be given the maximum sentence for first degree murder.

I looked at Mama and smiled, knowing that she had discovered the real menace back in September, long before the trial had begun.

By the third day of the trial, the preliminaries were over, and all the prosecution witnesses had testified. The prosecution had rested its case.

The judge turned to Mr. Jacoby, "Is the defense ready to begin its case?"

Mr. Jacoby rose to his feet. He wore a blue serge suit, and as usual dandruff flowed down his shoulders. Mama and I sat in the front row, watching him with eager anticipation to see how he used the evidence that Mama had uncovered.

"Yes, Your Honor," Mr. Jacoby said, turning to the judge. "I'd like to call my first witness."

The judge nodded his approval.

"I'd like to call Coroner Samuel Johnson back to the stand," Mr. Jacoby said.

Mr. Johnson returned to the stand. He had already been sworn in since he had testified for the prosecution.

174

In his earlier testimony, the coroner had stated that, upon his arrival at the scene of the crime, he had found that Harold Young had been shot three times through the back. His testimony, combined with the evidence presented by the ballistics experts, tended to prove incontrovertibly that Cheryl LaFlamme had shot Young. The ballistics evidence was that the gun, owned by Cheryl LaFlamme, had been the weapon used in the shooting and that parrafin tests proved Cheryl had powder residue on her hands and therefore must have pulled the trigger.

Mr. Jacoby began by saying, "I don't intend to question your earlier testimony. Instead, what I would like to know is how you handled Harold Young's body when you arrived at the scene of the crime?"

The coroner looked surprised. "We handled it the same way we handle all murder victims," he said.

"Would you kindly tell the jury how you handle all murder victims?" Mr. Jacoby asked.

"First," he said, "we take detailed photographs. We make notes about their physical attributes. We use a chemical thermometer to take the temperature of the room, then of the body."

"Can the temperature pin down the exact time of death?" Mr. Jacoby asked.

"No," the coroner answered, shaking his head. "Time of death is more elusive than most people think."

"Go on," Mr. Jacoby said.

"I look for traces of evidence that might not survive a trip to the morgue," he said.

"What happens to the body after that?" Mr. Jacoby asked.

"We gently place it on a stretcher and transport it to

the morgue."

"What do you do with the body at the morgue?"

"With a pencil-sized laser wand, we explore the flesh of the victim, looking for anything unusual or abnormal."

"What did you find on Harold Young's flesh?" Mr. Jacoby asked.

"Nothing," the coroner answered.

"Nothing?"

"There was nothing on the victim's flesh that was abnormal or out of place. I mean, there were no fibers, metals, chemicals, or dyes to indicate that something had contacted or entered the body through his skin abnormally."

"What did you do with the body after that?"

"We put it into the refrigerator."

"Did you perform an autopsy on the body?" Mr. Jacoby asked.

"Yes," the coroner said. "I performed the autopsy personally."

"What did you find?"

"Besides the fact that he had been shot three times?"

"Yes," Mr. Jacoby said. "Other than the fact that Harold Young had been shot three times."

"When I worked on his coronary arteries, I found that he hadn't been in the best of health," the coroner answered.

"In what way?" Mr. Jacoby asked.

"He had atherosclerosis along the walls of his blood vessels that had completely blocked his coronary artery."

"Help us to understand what that means in layman's terms," Mr. Jacoby prompted.

"It means that he was a walking time bomb. He was due for a heart attack at any time," the coroner said.

The courtroom became noisy as people began talking in an undertone. The judge demanded order. Mama looked at me and smiled. Things quieted down a bit.

The judge looked at Mr. Jacoby. "Go on with your questioning," he said.

Mr. Jacoby smiled, and I absently brushed my shoulders, just in case I had dandruff that I didn't know about.

"No further questions," Mr. Jacoby said.

The coroner stepped down from the witness stand.

"Your honor," Mr. Jacoby said. "I have no further witnesses, but I do have evidence I'd like to present to this court that, I believe, will prove that there is reasonable doubt that Cheryl LaFlamme killed Harold Young. This evidence will be vital in my summation before the jury."

"Proceed," the judge said.

Mr. Jacoby had one of his assistants bring into the courtroom a cardboard box. Mama and I winced when he explained that his "careful examination" of Mr. Young's background had prompted him to request a court order to search Mr. Young's office at J. Higgins & Sons. Upon a careful search, he continued, it was discovered that the hollow base of the office clock was in fact a secret drawer. He wished to enter the contents of that secret drawer to this court as evidence.

The prosecuting attorney tilted his head and frowned, not sure whether to object or not.

Mr. Jacoby slowly took out the first item. It was a large book, almost the size of Mama's old bible. "This, Your Honor and ladies and gentlemen of the jury," he said, in a powerful voice, "is a detailed account of the past twenty-five years of the late Harold Young's life. In his own handwriting, he chronicles how he stalked, raped, and killed one young child each year for that period of time." He paused, then added, "Or at least succeeding for twenty-four of those years. One child survived: the defendant, Cheryl LaFlamme."

There was an audible gasp from the spectators in the courtroom, followed by a murmur.

Mr. Jacoby faced the jury and spoke softly. "He confesses to these crimes in his own handwriting. *And....*" He raised his hand, and his voice resounded, "*he got away with it totally undetected!*"

Again a murmur ran through the courtroom. The prosecutor shot to his feet and snapped, "Objection, Your Honor! Relevancy! This is evidence of the victim's character and not germane to the question of the guilt or innocence of the accused!"

"Order!" the judge shouted, hitting his gavel to the desk. "Order in this courtroom!"

After a few minutes, order was restored.

"Mr. Jacoby," the judge said, "are you prepared to show that this evidence is relevant to the guilt or innocence of your client?"

"Yes, Your Honor," Mr. Jacoby said. "In my closing argument, I intend to use this evidence not only to show that there were mitigating circumstances for my client's going into the victim's office with a gun but also to provide a reasonable doubt that my client, Cheryl La Flamme, did indeed murder Mr. Young."

"Objection overruled," the judge said.

Mr. Jacoby continued. "I've shared these records with the police. And, if necessary, they are willing to testify to the accuracy of Mr. Young's records," he said, passing the diary to the judge, who scanned the pages, frowning in concentration, as the defense continued.

"These agencies," Jacoby said, "have scrupulously checked cases and have identified each and every one of Young's victims. The families of these victims can be satisfied that the monster who took their children away is no longer walking the streets of this city."

The judge suddenly stopped Jacoby and called a recess to allow time for him, the jury, and the prosecuting attorney to look through the diary.

Forty-five minutes later, Mr. Jacoby was back before the court. "You have seen, ladies and gentlemen," he said, "that by his own account, Mr. Harold Young was a child molester and murderer."

He pulled from the box a packet of maps held together with rubber bands. "These maps were used by the late Mr. Young to select his victims and stalk them in their own neighborhoods. Again, we've released this information to local police authorities. They are prepared to testify before this court, if necessary."

The courtroom was abuzz again.

"Order in this court!" the judge demanded. "If I hear one more such outburst," he said, "I will clear the courtroom and bar visitors from future proceedings."

Mr. Jacoby reached into the box and brought out a stack of pornographic magazines and handed them to the judge, who frowned when he discovered that they all depicted children engaged in sexual acts with each other and with adults.

"Mr. Jacoby," the judge said grimly, "are you saying that these magazines were with the diary in Mr. Young's office?"

When Mr. Jacoby acknowledged that this was correct, Judge Henderson asked him and the prosecuting attorney to approach the bench. After speaking to them briefly in a subdued voice inaudible to the spectators in the courtroom, the judge recessed the court for the day.

Chapter 21

Thursday, December 7

The next morning the judge announced that it had been agreed between the prosecuting and the defense attorneys that closing arguments could be presented to the jury.

"Mr. Prosecutor," Judge Henderson stated, "if you are ready, begin your closing argument, please."

The prosecuting attorney rose and began speaking: "Ladies and gentlemen of the jury, I know that my colleague, Mr. Jacoby, has presented evidence that has cast the victim, Harold Young, in a very damaging light. The man was a menace who should have been brought to justice years ago. I am not here to defend Harold Young's honor. On the contrary, the man died without honor. Nevertheless, we live in a democracy that stipulates that every human being, whether they are as despicable as Harold Young was, or as honorable as

Cheryl LaFlamme appears to be, deserves a trial by jury. We have courts to try and convict criminals, ladies and gentlemen, and Mr. Young has not been tried and convicted. That is not the issue today. I am here to address the issue.

"The facts show that Cheryl LaFlamme, maliciously and deliberately, stalked Harold Young, then went into his office and shot him three times in the back. You may consider whether or not she was in her right mind when she did this. That is your privilege. However, it is undeniable that she committed the act, and that is what she is on trial for in this court today. Ballistics showed that the bullets from her gun entered Harold Young's body from the rear. The fact is that the defendant shot and killed a man. Our laws demand that she be punished for this crime, a crime as serious as the ones Harold Young may have committed. I can say this, ladies and gentlemen," he continued, "because the crime of taking another human life is the most hideous of all crimes. It is an atrocity that can't be reversed and cannot be tolerated in a civilized society."

The courtroom was so quiet it was as if time had stopped.

"So," the prosecutor continued, "remember the issue that is before you today. Remember that this woman walked into a man's office and shot him to death. That is what this court is to judge. Nothing more and nobody else. Thank you."

Mr. Jacoby rose to present the closing argument for the defense: "Ladies and gentlemen, my colleague has stated accurately our position in this case. The issue that you are here to judge is whether or not Cheryl LaFlamme did in fact murder Harold Young. The judge has made it clear that you must come to this conclusion without any reasonable doubt. I propose to you, ladies and gentlemen, that there is a reasonable doubt.

"Let us recollect, if you will, exactly what happened on the day that Cheryl LaFlamme shot Harold Young. First of all, she called his office, and he refused to speak to her directly on the telephone. Secondly, when she arrived at his office, the testimony is that he said something that *sounded* like 'come in,' so the defendant walked into Harold Young's office.

"Keeping those facts in mind in addition to the atrocities that Harold Young had not only committed but documented, let us see what possibly happened to Harold Young on that fateful day.

"Harold Young was a child molester, a rapist, a killer. His diary presents proof that he had raped the defendant when she was five years old, but he did not succeed in killing her. Now, she accidentally runs into him on a airplane. At first, he doesn't recognize her, just as she doesn't recognize him. But, as her memory is prodded, so is his. He realizes, perhaps before she does, who she is, and he hurriedly leaves his vacation to return home. Now we know that he didn't do much work, though he gave an appearance of doing so. It is evident that his work was not the reason he cut his trip short. He recognized Cheryl and wanted to get away from her before she recognized him and remembered what he had done to her.

"Months pass; his record shows he is in the process of stalking his next victim. Ladies and gentlemen, Harold Young was not your typical psychotic. Most psychotics kill because of compulsion, an attempt to fill some need. The more he does it the stronger this

183

need becomes and the more frustrated he gets; therefore the stronger the urge will become. He becomes increasingly desensitized and it takes more with each killing to satiate his appetite. The satisfaction is temporary. Over the subsequent days and weeks, the tension builds until he finds his next target, stalks her, and kills her. The intervals between each killing may get shorter, and his activities may escalate.

"Not so with Harold Young. He was above average in intelligence, an obsessive-compulsive, and very organized and meticulous. He had to have an absolute control over his environment. And he calculated that, if his victims had no physical characteristics in common and that if he indulged himself only once a year, he could go on satisfying his desire for a long period of time. And, as horrible as it may seem, ladies and gentlemen, he was right.

"His diary corroborates what I've just said to you. Now, this egomanic finds out that he has a heart ailment. Medical records in evidence show that he knew six months before his death that he had serious heart problems. It was probably the reason he agreed to accompany his wife on the vacation. Of course, recognizing Cheryl LaFlamme didn't help his heart much, did it?

"He returns to his office and begins planning his yearly sacrifice, all the while becoming increasingly ill. I didn't put his wife on the stand, but in a deposition, she admits that her husband had been in very poor health for the last six months of his life.

"On the day that Cheryl LaFlamme calls his office, he is terribly ill, perhaps dying. His secretary tries to put the call through, but he is too ill to talk to her. He tells his secretary to have her come to his office about one o'clock. Why?

"He knows he is dying. The last irony, the ultimate insult. She will find his body; she will not get her revenge. He will go to the grave denying his only living victim the peace of mind of seeing him brought to justice.

"It is one o'clock. Cheryl LaFlamme arrives at Young's office. The secretary notifies him that she is in the outer office. With his dying breath, he tells her to come in. At that moment, ladies and gentlemen, Harold Young dies, satisfied that he has not been brought to justice. Cheryl LaFlamme walks into his office and begins talking to him. His back is to her, his face toward the window. He does not turn around, he does not speak…. He is dead. She shoots him in the back three times.

"I contend, ladies and gentlemen, that Cheryl LaFlamme shot Harold Young in the back three times, *but she did not kill him!* He was already dead. He died of natural causes, a massive heart attack. Now, if you were trying Cheryl LaFlamme for shooting Harold Young, then she is indeed guilty. But, ladies and gentlemen, that is not the charge that the State of Georgia has filed against Cheryl LaFlamme. They claim that she *killed* Harold Young. I say that there is a reasonable doubt that she did such a thing. I say that Harold Young was *already* dead several minutes before Cheryl LaFlamme pulled the trigger on the handgun she possessed.

"The only reason," Mr. Jacoby's voice dropped, "that Harold Young did not speak to Cheryl LaFlamme on the telephone the morning she called him was because he was too sick to talk to her. And the only reason Harold Young didn't turn around and speak to her that afternoon when she walked into his office was because he was already dead.

"Remember, ladies and gentlemen, there must be no reasonable doubt. The coroner testified that Harold Young could have had a heart attack at any time. His wife's deposition testified that he was extremely ill during the last six months of his life. His personal physician has stated that he refused the needed surgery for his condition."

Mr. Jacoby stepped up to the jury box and rested one elbow on it. "I contend, ladies and gentlemen, that in the twisted mind of Harold Young, he hated women. According to birth records, for the first five years of his life he was a little girl. Maybe he was jealous of other little girls' virginity. For whatever reason, the man dedicated his life to hurting and destroying them. And, as in life, facing death he played out the same scenario by trying to hurt Cheryl LaFlamme. His plan: she would find him dead and never gain revenge for the outrage that he had performed on her when she was five years old. He had no idea that she had a gun and that she was prepared to kill him. He had no idea, ladies and gentlemen, that she would be tried for his murder. Knowing what we now do of Harold Young, if he had realized that Cheryl would be tried and might be convicted for his murder, he would have felt that he had died with honor."

Mr. Jacoby turned his back to the jury and remarked as if he were speaking to himself: "I must keep myself from getting carried away by this case."

Then he turned around and once again addressed the

jury. "Remember," he said, his voice deep and pleasant. "The prosecution must prove guilt beyond a reasonable doubt. It must be proven that Harold Young died from the gunshots inflicted by Cheryl LaFlamme and not by a fatal heart attack!"

Mr. Jacoby went to the defense bench and sat down.

The courtroom was silent.

The judge cleared his throat several times to regain the attention of the jury. Then he instructed the jury on the points that they were to consider in coming up with a verdict and permitted them to retire to the jury room for their deliberations.

Chapter 22

The dining room table was set with Mama's hand-made lace tablecloth, her best china, and her crystal.

The food: fried chicken, turkey and dressing, collard greens, corn bread, pickled beets, homemade yeast rolls, glazed carrots, potato salad, field peas and okra, and rice. On the dessert tray there was red devil cake, sweet potato pie, and apple dumplings.

There were the seven of us: Cheryl, Mama and Daddy, Donna and Ernest, Cliff and me. We were celebrating Mama's victory. Even though Cheryl had shot him, she was found not guilty of murdering Harold Young.

On the other case Mama had been trying to resolve, Reverend Jones had turned himself in when he found out that his son had been put in prison.

And both Mama and I got huge bonuses from my

grateful employer, Mr. Sidney Jacoby.

"Why didn't the coroner figure out that Harold had died minutes before he was shot?" Cliff asked.

Mama smiled. "When the coroner arrived on the scene, the evidence and circumstances supported Harold's death by shooting. It was reasonable to assume when he performed his autopsy that Harold's heart condition was of little significance since he had been shot."

"I thought an autopsy could determine exactly how somebody had died," Ernest said.

"Not really," Mama replied. "An autopsy can't determine with one-hundred-percent certainty the time of death or the manner of death. The coroner uses the available evidence and circumstances to draw conclusions. Despite Young's bad heart, the circumstances and the evidence prompted the coroner to assume that Harold died of gunshot wounds rather than a heart attack."

"What did Mrs. Young tell you when you visited her?" Cheryl asked.

"She told me that Charlotte Young had confided to her that, when Harold was born, his sexual organs appeared to be female and he was treated like a girl until he turned five. At that time, his male organs descended. She knew something went wrong in his head, and that's why he had this fixation with little girls.

"Anyway, Irene Young said she had suspected him of child molestation for many years, but she was afraid of him. Right after their wedding, she became pregnant. When she told him, he beat her so badly that she had a miscarriage. He vowed never to do it again and begged her to become sterilized. She did. After that, she said, he insisted on her shaving all the hair from her body before they would have sex, so she would seem like a little girl.

"When he died, she said she found personal clothing, ribbons, scarves, and other items that belonged to the victims. Even though Harold had assaulted these girls, she couldn't go to the police with these items. After I talked with her, she did turn them over to the police, and they found them helpful in identifying the girls Harold had killed.

"She also said that Harold's health had been bad for the past few years. He'd had several mild heart attacks, but he had refused surgery. She was sure that he had agreed on the Bahamas vacation because he knew that he was dying. She didn't want you to be punished for his death, Cheryl, but she felt helpless to do anything. She had pleaded with Charlotte not to press the matter, but it didn't do any good. His sister didn't know about Harold's obsession, and Irene said she didn't have the heart to tell her what she suspected."

Cheryl leaned back in her chair. "She could have done something," she said.

"She didn't know what to do. After our first conversation, I sensed there was more she wanted to tell me but didn't know how to begin. That's why I had to talk to her again."

"How did she help you?" Cheryl asked.

She smiled at Cheryl. "It confirmed my suspicion that Harold Young was a dead man *before* you shot him."

"What made you suspect that?" Donna asked.

"The fact that he did not turn around and face Cheryl or speak to her when she came to confront him. From what I had gathered about Harold Young, he was not a timid man; he would have relished the confrontation. I figured he knew he was dying when Cheryl called, and that's why he didn't talk to her over the phone but actually asked her to come to his office."

"Did he want Cheryl to kill him?" I asked.

"No," Mama answered. "He had no idea that Cheryl had a gun or that she was considering shooting him. He simply wanted her to find him dead. He wanted her to see that she could not hurt him, just as he had made sure that the other little girls he had molested could never hurt him. It was all a part of his conceit."

"What do you mean?" Cheryl asked.

"Harold Young was a conceited, arrogant killer. Knowing that he was dying, his final act of violence was for *you* to see him escape punishment for what he had done to you. He probably laughed secretly to himself because he knew that the law would never be able to catch him or punish him for his crimes. He was dying of natural causes."

"Why didn't he call his doctor?"

"Again, I'm speculating, but he probably wanted to die. The one thing Harold Young dreaded was to be found out and punished for his deeds. In death, he would face no consequences for his actions."

Cliff coughed. "You figured him out."

Mama leaned forward. "Harold Young's wife, his secretary, the cleaning woman, and Cheryl all hinted that he was physically sick."

"What has happened to Charlotte Young?" Cheryl asked.

"I don't know," Mama said. Then she turned to look at me seriously. "By the way, Simone, I heard from your brother Rodney the other day."

"What's up with the folks in Jacksonville?" I asked.

"Everybody is fine, but Rodney suggested that there was something going on in his mother-in-law's neighborhood that we might find interesting."

"I can't believe that my brother is suggesting we take on a case?"

"He sounded skeptical. You know, I think he's impressed with our success in these two cases." She smiled. "Anyway, I told him that the problem would have to move to Atlanta before we could handle it."

"Well, be that as it may," my father said, leaning back in his chair and rubbing his stuffed belly, "you've outdone yourself this time, Candi. You've really outdone yourself with this meal."